David,

Simply stated,

I love you.

Enjoy!

Jane Ariel

READY TO MALE

A Collection of Letters

Lamar Ariel

authorHOUSE®

AuthorHouse™
1663 Liberty Drive, Suite 200
Bloomington, IN 47403
www.authorhouse.com
Phone: 1-800-839-8640

First published by AuthorHouse 9/15/2008

ISBN: 978-1-4389-0389-7 (sc)

Library of Congress Control Number: 2008908078

Printed in the United States of America
Bloomington, Indiana

This book is printed on acid-free paper.

This book is dedicated to *me*.

Hell, I wrote it.

AUTHOR'S NOTE

About a year ago, it seemed as though not one of the many thoughts bicycling through the maze in my brain ever reached a path that would allow them to exit. So one day, during one of my routine heart-to-heart conversations with myself, I said, "Care Bear (because you can address yourself however you might like), you have to find a way to stop all this traffic racing in your head."

A few days later, I was in the process of clearing off my desk when I uncovered an old cover letter. It totally made me laugh as I remembered the amount of time I had spent crafting 500 words to make the "Lizard of Oz," hiding behind an e-mail address, pick the *idea* of me versus someone else. After a few giggles and grunts of reflection, I decided to take a five-minute break from the two-minutes of cleaning I had just begun. During my downtime, I opened the cover letter file on my computer and tweaked the contents of the letter as if it were being written to a potential boyfriend. The new cover letter was addressed to *Dear Mr. Presumed Guilty.* And with my last pinky-fingered click of the enter key, I immediately e-mailed the letter to all of my friends.

After clicking "send," I received a phone call from a friend who was too busy laughing, on his side of the invisible line, to say "Hello." After he read aloud a few of the lines that "gagged" him the most, he made me promise to distribute a copy of that letter on all of my first dates. As we ended the conversation, he said, "Chile, they're not ready!" Laughing, I responded, "Neither am I!" When I hung up the phone, I replayed our conversation in my head and thought about the word *ready.* I wondered why I was excited to send that letter to my friends but clearly lacked the courage to deliver it to the person(s) for which it was actually intended.

Towards the end of the next week I wrote another letter that was more serious entitled *Dear How's Work?* This time, after e-mailing it to my friends, that same friend responded with an e-mail that read: "Lamar, this almost made me cry. You should most definitely <u>male</u> it to him." As simple as it was, his typo combined with my fascination with the word <u>ready</u> provided the basis for the name *Ready to Male* to be used as the title for the collection of letters you are about to read.

Ready to Male contains six chapters. Chapter One, "Is Easy Because You're Beautiful," contains letters written to and about the individuals who have taught and continue to teach me how to love. Chapter Two, "Find Him Keep Him, Lose Him Weep Him," consists of letters that uniquely document my emotions—depression, anger, loneliness, denial, and resolution—following the end of a tumultuous relationship. Chapter Three, "Creature of Bad Habits," describes the five types of men I have repeatedly dated during my ever-interesting existence as a single, gay man in New York City. Chapter Four, "Haughty Traveler," details some of my reflections and frustrations while using NYC's transit system. Chapter Five, "Very Perceptive, Practically Psychic," is a mix of social commentary and fantasy where I make certain predictions about my future and the future of America. And the last, Chapter Six, "Is It Me Or Is It New?" highlights some of my thoughts with regards to wanting, needing, and preparing for change.

As I sit and anxiously prepare to publish this first round of letters, I'd love to be able to tell you that my mind-traffic had finally slowed down, but that's just not the case. My thoughts—rebels that they are—pooled their coins together to buy a few motorcycles. And now, as they are able to drive faster and farther, I've constructed a few exit ramps in my maze that lead directly to an empty page. Enjoy!

TABLE OF CONTENTS

Dear God,

One day last week, I looked out my front window where I saw one of those cement trucks with the semi-oval-shaped drum turning clockwise. As I watched the truck, a construction worker wearing an orange hard hat and a neon-yellow vest pushed the truck's chute toward the area where cement was to be poured, and then pressed a button near the truck's taillight to release it. The man pressed the button again to stop the milkshake thick cement from flowing and proceeded to smooth over the ground where the cement was poured and block the area from foot traffic with a combination of yellow ropes and orange cones. When it was all done, he removed his hat and climbed into the passenger side of the truck as it drove away.

As soon as the construction workers left, a young boy raced toward the fresh cement with a broken broomstick in his hand as if he had been waiting for just the right opportunity. He kneeled near the drying cement and maneuvered his makeshift pen to scribble his name and draw a few squiggly lines underneath it. Even though there was a small part of me that wanted to raise the window and yell, "Stop that," I was stifled by my sincere empathy at his attempt to document his existence. You see, I believed that he—like me—wanted not only to share a part of himself but also preserve to it.

A few days later, I sat in front of my computer and decided to write a letter. I didn't really know what I wanted to say or to whom I wanted to say it to, but after about ten minutes of trying to insert the right word or phrase to replace the "?" following the "Dear," I typed the word "Me." When I looked at the page—empty except for those two words and a comma—I finally felt as though I had kneeled before the cement while the different layers of my identity—my emotions, my memories, and my dreams—used their own makeshift pen. In the time that followed that very special moment, they etched their first few lines.

After reading what had been written, I became unsettled because I could feel the burgeoning anxiety of other quiet feelings that wanted to tell their stories as well. As it was clear that one squiggly line simply would not do, I decided to provide all of them an opportunity to write. I didn't censor their words and I didn't even bother to confront them with my version of our shared thoughts and experiences. And with each sentence that appeared on a page, I learned things about myself that I couldn't have paid someone to teach me before. Their words allowed me to be more comfortable—just a little bit—with the complexity of existing as a simple human being.

God, it is my hope that this collection will inspire others to race toward those beautiful blocks of freshly laid cement. I just pray that you'll send me the special stamps I need to get these letters in the hands of those who will appreciate them the most.

Sincerely,
Lamar Ariel

CHAPTER ONE

Is Easy Because You're Beautiful

Dear Best Friend(s),

I distinctly remember being introduced to you by the mutual friend whom neither one of us speak to anymore, through an e-mail that our Dean of Pledges sent, while at my supervisor's house for his "white" party, when I was having drinks with my brother at that wine bar in Brooklyn, and on the first day of college. You were so masculine and handsome, cool and sweet, charming and funny, articulate and romantic, vibrant and fearless. My intrigue with your voice, humor, eyes, conversation, and energy was beyond immediate. As such, I guess it was no surprise that in the true tradition of gay-best-friendship, we had to experience a modicum of preliminary dating/courtship as well as primary ejaculation/sex all before concluding to just be friends. But that seems like eons ago—except for when I drink, haven't had "any" in a long time and you look really cute, or when you unexpectedly provide affection that reminds me that you are here to stay.

Remember the time you got so drunk that you threw up in that guy's car before he could merge onto the shoulder OR the time we went out in D.C. and danced like Alvin Ailey and Janet Jackson were watching OR the time we fearlessly went skinny dipping during that beach event in the Pines OR the time we got lost in Jersey trying to find something to eat after leaving the Juneteenth celebration OR do you remember the time your car spun off the road because of the black ice? And how about that time you convinced me to go to that dirty-ass bathhouse with you (so what if you left before I did) AND the time we went walking through the maze in Prospect Park AND the first time you showed me the picture of that boy who was going to have your ass on Dateline's *Catch a Predator* AND the time you started to date that boy you "met" in the park; AND how can we ever forget the time you were dating that psychotic bastard who claimed that I was the reason that you and his insecurities were having problems. I still laugh at: the memory of "je suis fatigue" at that restaurant in Montreal; my verbal assault on an unknown crazy woman in the street; the smell you released "that keeps the tops away" after another failed attempt to eat your hangover away; and the constant rolling of eyes as you conveniently directed rather than lifted any heavy boxes during your move. And one day it really won't be funny when I think about the time we did that E pill and you lost almost 20 pounds due to an allergic reaction.

And since we're strolling down memory catwalk, I am still mad about the time you went on gaycation without me; the embarrassing sight of your fem-vogue routine at Brooklyn Café; your lack of paternal instincts as I flirted and inadvertently disappeared with that ugly ass boy into the club bathroom; how you didn't come to the get-together I had when my mom was in town because "something came up" (just your penis as usual); and yes, I still get a little hot when I think about how my telephone number somehow finds its way in the contact list of every pitiful ass boy who's trying to get close to *you* through me. And while I'm at it, let us not forget about the fact that you continue to forbid me from screwing the boy known as "pure hotness" that you dated (three days don't count bitch); the fact that I still haven't met your damn mother; the irritating way in which you start off your description of new "boos" by describing how perfect they are for me; the fact that I still don't have a copy of your depression CD; and most sadly, the fact that your first and only attempt at matchmaking involved an arrogant and facially offensive gnome with a medical degree. So if by some chance you thought this letter was going to be sentimental, as you nauseatingly say, "chile, boo."

I would never share with you how I am convinced that your hugs are constant first dates wrapped in the ribbon of first kisses and handheld strolls. I am confident that your attention is a calming aromatic bath on a brutally cold winter day. My spirit knows that your ability to make me feel better and silly in the same breath is as remarkable as watching a wave dance against the shore. My soul remembers that your passion and intensity are as contagious as a yawn in an overcrowded elevator. I can't forget that your zest for life and ignorance to the existence of

IS EASY BECAUSE YOU'RE BEAUTIFUL

4

the word "regret" is the reason why suicide is the exception and not the rule. I will never run out of reasons to smile like we just counted down the seconds to a new year at the thought of you.

Just like *Tom* with *Jerry*, *The Brain* with *Pinky*, *Lilo* with *Stitch*, *Stewie* with *Brian*, and *Gin* with *Tonic*, I struggle because I realize that defining your role in my life is almost as complicated as explaining the meaning of life. You see, there are many days where I find myself sitting cross-legged on the floor as God teaches me the art of being human as I reflect upon *your* pain, *your* promise, *your* unconcern, *your* genius, and *your* freedom. I focus intently on each infinite moment of instruction and the resulting laughter, truth, importance, wit, and growth with a liturgical sensation and a sponge's personification. Truly grateful for the access to the insights you possess, I am often sympathetic toward the less fortunate whom have misguided beliefs regarding the utility of a mirror. Only paying attention to the obvious, they fail to value the difference between one's imitation, one's representation, and one's reality. It is far too unfortunate that, unlike me, when they look into that special glass, they don't see *you.*

Love Always,
Complete

Dear Because I Said So,

One hour before my lungs would breathe God's air for the first time, you stood on Mount Kilimanjaro waiting for the sun to rise. You were barefoot wearing a hooded sable fur coat with a celestial royal train. Decorated with red rose pedals, your beautiful brown hair flowed at the sides of your peachy yellow face as I waited anxiously inside your heart. As the sun began to rise, you glided to the highest point on the mountain to have a meeting with God, where He held you tightly for five minutes and then whispered in your ear for two—the secrets of being a phenomenal mother. Once done, you shed a tear that traveled the path from your eye to the corner of your mouth to your neck onto the center of your chest exactly at the moment when the sun rose from the sea—dripping wet with the blood of sacrifice and determination.

Simultaneously, the wise women who took care of me in your heart quickly kissed me goodbye as the eldest placed a 24-carat peridot amulet around my neck to protect me from the impending winds of life. Then suddenly, there was a flash of light and a blast of cold air as I exploded from your core. The force was so strong that I was propelled into the heavens, landing on a gold cumulus cloud where I was kissed by one million angels. White doves slowly circled above my head carrying the promises of success, encouragement, happiness, fearlessness, and most importantly, faith. After the last angel blessed me with a kiss, you soared to my cloud and claimed me—your little one—and as intended, we exchanged the legendary look into each other's eyes that consecrated our lifelong partnership as mother and son.

When I was young, I would often watch you spin into your Wonder Woman costume with sincere awe and admiration as you transformed the tired and evil half of your Gemini spirit into a radiant and sweetly perfumed teacher. Completely mesmerized, I wanted desperately to be as beautiful as you, as powerful as you, as loving as you, as in control as you, and as authentically unique as you. I wanted to be respected, to put family first while creatively stealing time for self, to have an opinion that others trusted, to be able to enjoy a good laugh during sadness and to have the ability to plan for tomorrow with a certain inexhaustible energy to get through "today." What a wonderful thing it was to observe how to be personable not loud, complex while appearing to be simple, happy despite the thoughts that could keep you mad, and how to remain artfully present for whatever the moment might bring.

Sometimes I ask myself, What would it be like to never feel loved? What would it be like to not feel valued and accepted? What would it be like to feel neglected? What would it be like to have low self-esteem? What would it be like to never hear the words *I love you?* What if no one had ever helped me with my homework? What would it be like to never be told I was smart? How would I understand what love is if you didn't show me? What if you never encouraged me to be artistic? What if you couldn't be real with me? What if you were weak? What if I didn't come first? What if I couldn't complain about you loving me too much, calling me too much, asking too many questions, always giving advice, and being overprotective? Do you know how appreciative I am that I will *never* know?

Love,
Your Grateful Little One

PS

<u>I heard loud and clear</u>—when you got a C on my report about birds for science class; when you told that teacher you couldn't kick her ass for not replacing the sunglasses she took from me and lost; when you took a half day from work each and every time I didn't feel good; when you sent money so that I could "treat myself to a nice meal"; when you mailed those unexpected greeting cards with a smiley face as well as a "miss you" in your unmistakable handwriting; when you never missed a spelling bee, dance recital, band or orchestra concert, fashion show, or any other opportunity to see me perform; when you ignored every adolescent temper tantrum I had; when you told me any

grade I got was fine as long as I tried my best; when you took me to Baskin Robbins for ice cream every Friday without fail; when you made an apple pie from scratch in order to prove that you could cook (if you wanted to); when you decided that you would respect my choice to love who I wanted to love; when you found me out of a crowd of thousands at college graduation and couldn't help but cry—the whispers of your love.

I will never forget—that we had breakfast with Santa Claus well after I had sprouted facial hair; the forced readings of *The Night Before Christmas* on Christmas Eve until I was in college; every birthday you treated like it was my first; the time I taught you how to do the electric slide in Jamaica; the conversations where you warned me about dating older men; the way you described your life having real meaning once I was born; the moment I started to cry (around eight years old) after imagining what would become of me if you were to die; the first time I cooked you dinner and stood outside your bedroom to hear you tell your friends how delicious it was; the look on your face when I bought you the puppy for your birthday; the moment I showed you the ring from Tiffany and you said, "You deserve it."—your hand on top of mine as you showed me how to write the word "Mother."

Dear How's Work?

Dad, I received a pale orange notecard from the United States Postal Service informing me that a third and final attempt to deliver certified mail had come to my address. When I turned the card over, I was stunned as well as curious to see your name and address. As I relocked my mailbox—oddly containing nothing more than this flimsy little notecard in it—I wondered intently about what you had sent. I mean, it wasn't my birthday nor was it Christmas, and quite honestly, even if it was, you and I both know that it would still be slightly peculiar to have mail from you. Not to say that you don't call or do things in your own way, but at least if it were a holiday, I would have a better idea of what it was that you sent.

Once in my apartment, I called the number printed on the card with hopes of retrieving the package from a nearby post office. Unfortunately, the office's automated phone system indicated they were already closed. Since your mystery package and I had to wait until tomorrow to be united, I started my after-work routine of opening a bottle of Sauvignon Blanc, lighting a scented candle, microwaving leftover Chinese food from the day before and playing my current favorite CD, *Feeling Orange But Sometimes Blue.* As I sat, enjoying the sight of life unconnected to a computer screen, my thoughts were drawn to the post card that I left on the kitchen counter. I stood up, grabbed the card from the counter and carried it back to the couch. I don't know if it was the wine or just the fact that I was exhausted from a very long day at work, but I found myself in a daze.

I began to think about the moments where I felt as if I were an extension of a man—of so many men—who, more often than not, I really knew very little about. They were the men in our family for whom I had questions—as a boy, as a teenager, and as a man—that were never directly answered. To be clear, there were times when my mother, grandmother, aunts, sister, or even female cousins would tell me things that they thought I should know about the men in our lives. And as well intentioned as they might have been, their answers always felt one-sided because they never came directly from the source. They never came directly from you.

Projecting my need for answers onto the mystery of this unexpected mail you sent, I began to think of all the things you could have written. I imagined that your mail was a letter full of answers that you'd written especially for me. Maybe you would share some of your thoughts: *Things you wanted me to know that you had to learn the hard way; family members you wish you had spent more time with when you were a child; a description of the first person you ever kissed and the way it made you feel; a story about the first girl you ever gave a flower to and the type of flower it was; the name of first person you ever slow danced with and who led whom; your thoughts on what makes a relationship work; the experience that taught you what love was and how it has changed over the years; the moment you proposed to my mother and what made you decide that she and the time were right; your reaction when you learned my mother was pregnant with me; how you felt the first time you held me in your arms; the first time I made you laugh; your favorite memory of me as a child; the first time I truly made you proud; the challenging parts about being a father and why it seems like you enjoy being a grandfather so much more*—about the things you learned about love.

My mind wandered. I thought that perhaps you'd open up about some of the difficult times of your life and provide narrative about the pain. Maybe you'd answer questions like: *When was the first time you cried? Who was the first person to ever break your heart and how long did it take you to get pass that feeling? When was the first time you cheated in a relationship and when was the first time you got caught? Why don't you think your marriages lasted any longer than they did? What's the hardest part about ending a relationship? Who or what disappointed you the most in life? What was the angriest moment in your life and how did you handle it? Does almost ever count?*

And, while you were sharing, maybe you'd finally provide some insights into your thoughts about sex. *Do you have any sexual regrets? How old were you the first time you were intimate and what song was playing in the background? When was the first time you made love and how did you know it was different from just having sex? Did you ever stop separating the two? Is sex different as a mature adult compared to when you are young? What didn't your father teach you about sex that you had to learn on your own? Is it safe to assume that, unlike me, you never had a thought about being gay?*

Honestly, it was as if all of my thoughts transformed themselves into a blur of never-ending questions. I even wondered about the miscellaneous things—*the best party you ever went to, the dumbest thing you ever said or did, the best book you ever read, the name of your favorite song, the hardest thing about being you, the moment you realized you were no longer young, your biggest concerns about the world today, the things you did wrong as a parent and the things you know you did right, your definition of a man, the one thing you believe could make the world a better place, the real meaning of being a Black man in America, the influence your children have had on the way you view the world, the things you would do differently knowing what you know now*—about your life. I was consumed.

My brain had been so overworked that finally I just fell asleep. And when I woke up the next morning, now anxious, I couldn't wait to get to the post office to pick up your package. As I walked to the post office, the possibility of organizing the pieces of the puzzle that would allow me to get to know the real you fascinated me. Would I learn things about you that would help me enjoy versus avoid our similarities? Could I finally remove the "about" that stood between me simply knowing you?

For the first time ever, I believed in my heart that I wanted those answers to be YES. I recognized the importance of knowing *you*.

When the postal worker behind the window handed me the thick, padded envelope, I instantly knew I was completely wrong about your mail. The letter I wanted didn't require padding it just required care. In hindsight, it was totally my fault; and I really had no one to blame but myself. I should have just waited to actually pick up the package rather than create some unrealistic letter in my head.

I'm sorry for rambling. I just wanted to say congratulations and extend thanks for the pictures of your new summer home in Florida. I'll definitely frame a few of them. I'm looking forward to seeing it in person one day when things at work slow down.

Love,
One Who Should Know You Better

Dear Grace,

"Five little monkeys, jumping on the bed, one fell off and bumped his head. Mama called the doctor, and the doctor said, No-more- jumping- on-the-bed. Four little...." On the school bus, surrounded by what I then considered Neanderthal little boys and girls, I impatiently sat tapping my fingers on my knee as I awaited the daily yet long-overdue feeling that comes with being home from school. My school day consisted of unvarying *"yo mama"* jokes, being picked on and bullied by older gay boys who wanted to experiment (confirmed when I stumbled upon these butch queens at the *club* this year), and the rock-steady prepubescent lovebirds who were always tongue kissing each other the way they had learned from *The Wonder Years*. Needless to say, I couldn't wait to get home.

Exiting that school bus every afternoon was a calm breath after climbing several flights of stairs—no matter how many times it happened, it still felt pretty damn good.

Once home, I would perform a quick costume change into festive playground attire, overfeed my soon-to-be-in-fishy-heaven fish, and then run through my middle-class neighborhood, past the basketball court, past the *He-man* action figures, past the countdowns of hide-and-seek, and past the stares, to my very first taboo activity—double Dutch. At first, I used to just lean against a nearby tree and watch. However, this all changed one day when you asked me if I wanted to jump. Initially, I pretended to be disinterested because I thought it was bad *enough* that I was the only boy standing around watching a "girl sport." I was convinced that jumping rope, especially double Dutch, would be like wearing a moving neon sign that confirmed my already pretty obvious truth. Yet and still, after an intense 10-second persuasion—*"I know you want to, it's okay, boys can double Dutch, too"*—I would never be the same. Double Dutch was more fun than anything I had experienced: thin, white rope rhythmically and individually chasing my feet, songs that were sung either to make me lose or keep concentration (still can't decide), and the sensation of gravity courageously being fought by cute little me. With our Cross Colours jeans worn backwards, our insanely long conversations about all the things/people we'd do if we were adults, our years believing that we were aliens sent to observe the human race, and all of our time spent sharing "top-secret" girls-only and boys-only stuff. We became inseparable.

"Dribble it (clap, clap); Pass it (stomp, stomp); Dribble it, Pass it, We Want a Basket (toe-touch)" During our freshman year of high school, I became privy to your untrained magical power of identifying and befriending boys like me. As an only child who had never liked to or been forced to share his toys, I must admit that, initially, I was quite jealous. You were my beautiful doll whose hair I never had to sneak to comb, brush or braid, which meant a lot to a boy from a family of women obsessed with hair but not exactly comfortable letting their sons and grandsons take their "look" to the next level.

Thankfully, a few hours after the chemistry class in which I neurotically convinced myself that my gift from God and the only person who truly "got me" was sharing her friendship with other up-and-coming gays, the unthinkable happened: Your first boyfriend inadvertently became my first sexual experience. There I was, minding my own damn business in *his* car, when your teenage boyfriend asks me if he could "see" it. And as the ageless story of teenage hormones goes: feel, taste, smell, and see it he did. We tried to keep it a secret for a while (three days) until I re-realized how wrong it was and therefore needed to come clean. That's why I made him tell you he was gay and that he wanted to be with me. By the next week, everything was resolved. You forgave me, I stopped "playing" with him, and he got back with his ex-girlfriend.

Sadly (for you), even though this love triangle left you guarded about your taste in boys, it would take you quite some time to recognize that you were confusing your untrained feelings with your fetish. Hell, it was almost as if you had dedicated your teenage years to handpicking my jump-offs. In fact, it became so regular that I discovered a formula: *You + Boy*

You Really Love = My New Freak[2]. There was the percussionist, the cheerleader (girl please), the *wanna-be* hip-hop entrepreneur, the weed head (should have known he was escaping some demons), and even the nerd (ok, fine, I turned him out). They all thought I was mad cool, *hella* funny, or any number of countless descriptions that all translated into "I'm completely pressed to see your best friend naked." Now to be clear, not all of them had the pleasure of *having* the pleasure. But girl, due to your "gaydar" running amuck, my high-school years were a collection of literal and nonliteral blasts!

   "You wish you had a nickel, you wish you had a dime, you wish you had an AKA to love you all the time. You wish you had a quarter, you wish you had a dollar, you wish you had an AKA to make you scream and holler." When we arrived in college, I knew it was only a matter of time before you would join *the* sorority. After all, it's what girls like you who fancy boys like me tend to do! It seems like only yesterday that I distinctly remember all of your greedy, nasty, loud, and skank-ass line sisters coming by the apartment for what would be the last moment, for a long time, that your first name wouldn't be followed by "the AKA." With my hand on my hip and an evil eye staring at your, "she just-big-boned" line sister (wanted to fight this whore several times for always eating the last of something), I stood in the background as only an incredibly proud gay best friend can. My Grace would finally be able to publicly become the bitch I had grown to know and love. On a quick side note, had your no-talent Dean of Pledges, *Big Sister Pink and I Don't Eat Enough Greens*, had the foresight to let me choreograph your coming-out show, the campus would STILL be talking about how fierce your line was! But I digress, it was still very *cute*: your green-apple-green pumps, your shoulder length hair snapping from side to side, that ever-so-aggravating dolphin mating call, and that soon to be infamous pinky finger raised high in the bourgeoisie collegiate air. You were always beautiful to me, but somehow after this moment, I guess I was officially made aware that you were *pretty!*

Once we became working adults, I decided that the word "hag" was an inappropriate label for such an incredibly meaningful person in my life. After I considered the day I told you I was gay and your undelayed as well as unbothered (*"And?"*) response; T.G.I. Friday's after that "hell-I-can-barely-afford-me" trip to the abortion clinic; the unforgettable moment in church when we saw that the new preacher was F-I-N-E; sitting in the park playing God as we created stories about the unwritten comedies who passed us by; listening to you answer questions in class and wondering if you knew how freakishly smart you were; the wedding toast you gave for our public-speaking class that made me cry; driving to Popeyes on Friday afternoons and eating chicken like it was the last time we ever could; the *aww* look that the sweet elderly black woman gave us while we were shopping for Thanksgiving dinner; eating those weed brownies and being high for three days (including the day we had to go to class); drinking cheap wine and watching the *Law & Order* overnight marathons with brief calls during the commercial breaks; and all of the completely pornographic conversations we have had about the men we would never marry—it was clear to me that I had to find a much better title for you.

Unfortunately, my little, cinnamon bunny who's made of more naughty than nice, I'm not having a lot of luck finding an appropriate term of endearment. So Grace, until I invent the right word, I hope you are comfortable just being *amazing!*

Love Always,
Wretch Like Me

CHAPTER TWO

Find Him Keep Him, Lose Him Weep Him.

Dear Bright Eyed and Bushy Tailed,

My bed is a garden: dirt, buried memories, and dandelions of unwanted emotions. The ceiling is the sun: desert hot, out of reach, fulgent, and powerfully suppressive. The sounds of footsteps above the sun—heel to toe, proud, heavy, and unapologetic—are just like the ones I plan to make after I outgrow my soil. A lukewarm breeze from outside of the slightly cracked window next to my garden whispers across my face—kids laughing, help on the way sirens, trucks carrying packages, aircraft taking off and cars speeding somewhere fun—sounding meaningless promises of more meaningful days. Something electric clicks strangely and scares me into waking up. *"Who's there? Am I dead yet? Am I alive still? Where...am...I?"*

I walk into the bathroom and look at this oddly familiar person in the mirror and begin to wonder how *he* got there. After about five minutes, I stop him from staring at me by sliding the medicine cabinet door to the left. I grab a big blue container of face cleaner that my mother taught me to use, open it in a counterclockwise motion, place the lid on one side of the bathroom counter and the contents on the other. I force two trembling fingers to the bottom of the container, scoop out more than I should and then slide the cabinet door back to the right. With artistic strokes, I paint my face, covering the invisible, hiding what's clear, bleaching my colors until I eerily become the shadow of the man that is now crying as *he* looks back at me. My hands throw water in his face. Splash. Splash. His hands throw water back at mine. We are even. We stare at each other as the water runs downward and the sensation of warm skin meeting colder-than-expected liquid travels up. *Is he going to be okay? Who should move first? Will he stop me from staring at him so intensely?"*

It takes ten blinks of my eyes and five steps to turn on the shower. I apprehensively step in and close the glass shower door behind me. Eyes closed—pump, pump, pump on the shampoo—I turn my back to the showerhead and allow the water to concentrate on my neck as I scratch my scalp. I turn around to grab the barely there bar of lemon-mint soap and casually take it for an uninteresting tour of my depression-scented body. First stop, my volcanic stomach and all of its sulfuric contents that help me to sleep at night. Next stop, the haunted castle between my legs whose recent visitors have either not paid or sent checks that bounced. After quick tours of other grassy areas, we end at our final destination, my feet. Leaning over and unsuccessfully trying to balance the weight on my shoulders, I decide to just sit down and massage my feet with the last scrap of soap. The warm water pours over my head and like a heavy rain it sometimes forces me to gasp for breath and open my eyes. The last sliver of soap melts away from my hand. My skin is clean yet I still feel dirty. *"Why don't I want to stand up? How do I clean my mind? How do I change the way my heart smells?"*

The water turns cold, so I step out so that the oversized bath sheet and I can find each other. Avoiding *that* man, I walk past the mirror and begin to dress: mismatched socks, last pair of clean underwear, long sleeve dress shirt, dress slacks, belt and finally, shoes. I stroll to the kitchen and I pour myself a small glass of grapefruit juice and infuse it with a larger amount of vodka. I chug it along with a medium-large slice of triple chocolate cake and as my blood sugar rises, I look at the microwave clock and realize that I'm more than thirty minutes late for work.   I brush my teeth at the kitchen sink so that I don't have to look at *him* again; and quickly gargle, spit, and wipe my mouth with a paper towel. I grab my house keys and iPod then place them in my workbag. I put my hat and coat on me, their hue-mannequin, and then make a quick dash into the bathroom in order to allow *him* to spritz me with cologne. I snatch my scarf from its resting place on the floor, wrap it around my neck, and grab my belongings in the seconds before the morning's pain is securely contained behind me. I lock my apartment door with four keys, run down three flights of steps, and slam two doors as I exit my brownstone. Slapped by the brisk cold, I swiftly make my descent down the steps while simultaneously placing my iPod earplugs in their respective canals and press play just before I reach the last step. I begin walking toward the train and catch a glimpse of the *other* sun and recognize that it is, once again, another day that I somehow managed to get out of my bed. *"What is it like to love waking up? How does it feel to love, looking back at,* him?"

Sincerely,
Much More of a Night Person

Dear You Said You Loved Me,

As much as I thought/hoped/wanted to be your friend after our painful "divorce," you have shown me time and time again that it is impossible to be in your life without being constantly annoyed, aggravated, and utterly disappointed in you as well as your highly underdeveloped ability to be a *real* adult. Thanks be unto the Lord that *Dateline* didn't catch up with me because the producer clearly would have arrested me for trying to love your juvenile ass. So here it is, direct and to the point—your presence in my life is no longer warranted. I have often heard you say, "Life is too short to be unhappy," and overhearing it in the context of "why we didn't work out," as you joked with your friends, was certainly the loud "fuck you" I needed to let me know that you and whoever you stole that thought from (because you are too stupid to create anything on your own, including happiness) are indeed, one-million percent right. There is no need to be unhappy with some miserable, underachieving, static, and poorly bred parasitic shadow of a man. And unfortunately my dear, that happens to be all of the things I currently use to describe you.

Knowing you, God knows I do, you probably are wondering—"What did I do to do deserve this?" And guess what, for different reasons, so am I. According to Peaches, (President, United Ghetto Bitches of America), the first step in getting over a man is to make him feel like shit and then deal with your own stuff after you get laid a couple of times. Since I went in reverse order (started with sleeping with a few of your friends), I'm writing this letter to your sorry ass, now, that I have some free time.

I'll make it simple for you: I came to your birthday party—because I actually thought we were friends—and overheard you introduce the living antithesis of me as your "new" husband, and we haven't even been apart for three months. I'll repeat: I came to your birthday party and overheard you introduce the living antithesis of me as your "new" husband and we haven't even been apart for three months. To be fair, he is definitely cute and does seem more like your *type*. He looks just like somebody who won't love the real you. And that's perfect because it remains to be proven that, well, you do.

You have called me almost every other day during the past two months with a constant attack of what-do-you-think's; should-I-do-that's; can you proofread this's; and can you invite them's—all in relation to this party. Additionally, we have even had a few dinners and late-night "I-miss-you" conversations where I have specifically asked your lying ass if you were dating anyone to which you responded with ramblings of "so busy with work," "casually but nothing serious," and "taking time for me."

Now, as a self-described workaholic, noncommittal, selfish and might I add dysfunctional person: How in the hell do you find the time to find a new "husband" that you are ecstatic to introduce to your co-workers and friends? And, how dare you not inform me that this bastard existed and would be in attendance at the party that I helped your trifling ass plan? And before I was overcome with nausea and mad-bitch syndrome that night, why did you continue to engage me in your typical public displays of affection knowing that he was only steps away?

But all in all, it's all good (asshole). You don't even need to apologize—your life has enough moments of regret. And you certainly don't have to explain (motherfucker)—because I *just* figured it out. But by all means (shithead), keep your memories of my incredibly wholesome and supportive love, because you'll definitely need it! I no longer choose to allow you in my life. You simply DO NOT deserve to be there. You are nothing more to me than an infantile shell of a potential man that is clearly incapable of simply being a friend.

Finally (such a great word for letters like these), let us be clear—This is not about your new love! This is about YOU and your lack of RESPECT. I don't <u>want</u> you. I know you. I know your truth. I know your issues. I know the man you pretend to be.

Lose my address. Lose my number. Lose my e-mail.
You already loss your space in my life.
THE END...Of more than just this letter.

Sincerely,
Mad About It

Dear Funny Valentine,

I'm sorry about the letter I sent you a few days ago, but I've really been going through it since our relationship ended. Naively, I really didn't think I would or could miss you like this. I thought I'd be sad for a couple of days and just move on. I thought making the decision to end things would bury all of my disappointment and frustration into my garden of forget-him-yes's. I guess I convinced myself that control of my life would be regained by not having you in it. But despite my best efforts to control this longing, this craving, this yearning; it feels like there is a coup d'état happening inside me. My logical thoughts don't respect my emotions and my heart continues to ridicule and laugh at my brain's blatantly arrogant feeling of authority. Every speech I make to convince myself that we should just be friends quickly becomes laughable propaganda in the war I'm fighting to try *not* to want you. I can't hear me because all of the voices in my head are screaming your name. I can't see me because whenever I look into the mirror I see things like my daily teeth-brushing ritual made complete by your good morning nibble on the bottom of my ear. It seems as though all I can do is tearfully stumble through one blurry memory of you after the next. I know there is probably a much better way to say this, but baby, I miss you.

The texture of this whole experience is like sand. You see there are the pretty little pebbles that I'm trying to keep—those times where there was no confusion and no fighting between us—but they are unceremoniously slipping through my fingers. On the flip side, there are the slightly larger and more abrasive pebbles that I want to simply forget, like those unreasonable expectations that I created, but they leave a dark stain on both sides of my hands. And seriously, I can't even imagine building a new sand castle considering how much I mourn the one that my stupidity and judgmental ways just washed away. I know that it's only been three months but I really don't know how to say it any other way. I'm still not over you.

I'm ashamed to admit how I bought extra pillows so that I could pretend you were on your side of the bed; but no matter how creatively I stacked them, they couldn't sense when to hold me extra tight. I'm reluctant to tell you about the day I went to Baskin Robbins and ordered a quart of pistachio as well as Rocky Road ice cream, but as soon as I began my voyage into gluttony I realized it wasn't the same because you weren't there to tell me that the pink spoon is what really made the ice cream taste so good. I try to forget how I sometimes forget the fact that we broke up when I watch our favorite TV show and, out of habit, dial your number because I want to repeat all of the funny parts to make you laugh again. I feel like the lone survivor of so many small things that I took for granted while we were *we*. And now that I can't sleep or enjoy life the same way we used to, I want to get/have/feel you back in my life.

Now I know that you and that guy at your party are dating but I guess I'm hoping that things aren't that serious. I mean because if you are just getting to know him, I'd really like to see if we can make our relationship a reality again. I know you love me and you have to know that you are the one for me. I'm living in real time now and I know that no man or relationship is perfect.

I want you back in my life so that I can love all of your flaws and you can help me realize mine. Can you sign me up for the good days, the bad days, and the moments in between? I want to feel your hand in mine as we take a longer walk, a real walk. I know it might sound dramatic but my only need in life is to love you. I'm here. I'm begging you for an opportunity to make this work.

I want to be the better half of the only one who ever really reciprocated what they inspired me to give. I want you to let me show you how we can take our mistakes and transform them into answers. I want you to let our love give us a fresh start with only new moments filling our expectations. I don't want to miss you anymore. Please, just come back.

Sincerely,
Lost Without You

Dear Trying to Get Over His Ass,

I am so sorry to see that you are in pain right now. Unfortunately, due to your admitted over-zealousness as well as a few instances of half-heartedness towards potential partners, it appears as though you go out of your way to place yourself in this predicament over and over again. But its okay because you are only human and this, believe it or not, is what your twenties are unfortunately all about. I hope you will use this recap of your relationship with Hello/Goodbye as a means of emotive advancement rather than a rationale for prolonged detachment and despair. Remember, the key to finding love is to first locate it from within.

It seems as though only yesterday you were beaming with that all-too-familiar "cockiness" and semihallucinogenic sense of purpose that the seductive promise of a new love—the new "Mr. Right" love—can bring. You, with all of your special bath products, body oils, and French cologne/perfume, depending on your mood, were once again inspired to show the world, and him, what simple attributes—youth, naiveté, fearlessness—could herald in your new beginning. How tenderly you strolled through the grocery store with your headphones playing that old single spiritual "Way to His Heart," as you selected all of the key ingredients to make a feast that would fill his stomach and mind with recurring notions of "Could this be?" "Is he real?" and "Damn, he can cook." Yes, my loyal friend you were cooking a pot of love so strong that its intoxicating liquor alone would lull any mere human into the Negroidian slumber of commitment.

While he was peacefully sleeping in his adumbral state of commitment, you overlooked and redirected quite a few of his major life shortcomings. Without being too harsh on you as I know this is still a difficult process for you to manage (especially for someone as "edumacated" as you is) do realize that you fell in love with a man addicted to avoiding the big problems (pink elephants included), inhaling royal vagueness (purple haze), inciting unwarranted control, and irritatingly replacing function with dysfunction at every unexpected gap along the relationship road.

Overjoyed with his striking appearance and unconvinced of his unrealized potential, you allowed yourself to participate in many a Vaseline-faced hour of combat against the arguments of "hue versus fear," "not-right versus okay," "addiction versus most people do it," "I've just been busy versus let's talk about it right now," "I don't know versus I can't say it to you," "let's fantasize versus let's realize," "this is my special love versus we don't sleep together," "I will never let anything bad happen to you versus I will do as much as I am comfortable with to maintain your presence," and the one that I know hurt you the most, "I love you versus I love you, but...."

And yes, to be fair, he was not all bad. In fact, as the truth, I can confirm that he hypnotized you with his affection and charm, brought new excitement to the art of dessert, loved you with or without a job, held you the same despite a few extra pounds, enamored your face like a prized Serolla painting, valued your opinion on world topics, and even replaced your negative thoughts with positive affirmations. And let's not forget the way watching him articulate a sentence or engage a client/employer/friend would rush your thoughts to the cliff of "I could marry him." How the touch of his lips on the back of your neck followed by "this is the best part of my day" or the taste and motion of his tongue would lay wet in your mind for daze at a time, or the way his smile could turn your frown into smoldering tranquility, or how the palm of your hand followed the shape of his behind while you slept in his fortress of pillows, or how he could make a ten-dollar shopping spree one of the most romantic evenings of your life. Let's not even mention the many silly and ridiculously cute nicknames for you—Patch, My Little Boy, Pumpkin Head—that used to excite you like the thought of two weeks to graduation.

You have to realize that you chose to fall in love with he who could be everything but only wanted to be something. His silence, overcompensation, defensiveness, and general problem-hiding skills sang misplaced lyrics of "Neither One of Us," "Guess Who I Saw Today," "Go Away Little Boy," "Where Is the Love," and his namesake "Hello-Goodbye." Meanwhile, your regret in the way you ended your last relationship, want for something consistent in a constantly changing twenty-fifth year, as well as a crazy fixation on a biological clock (that hasn't even started to tick) kept you in a sandman-worthy performance containing lyrical highlights such as "No One Else," "Gotta Find a Way," "Just the Two of Us," and the curtain dropper "I Belong to You."

Understanding your misguided decision to wear paparazzi-defying sunglasses while night driving a semitruck on precarious relationship lane will allow you to clearly see the unavoidable crash of Hello/Goodbye. For whatever reason, this man/juncture in your life couldn't commit to the relationship in the same way you needed him to. Did he love you? Of course he did. Wouldn't you love the man who allowed you to shy away from the tough moments while giving you all of the love you could possibly need? Of course you would. In the end, you have to realize that fault was equal to both parties. You fed your fantasy, he fed his, and neither focused on nurturing the reality of the situation.

Metaphorically speaking, you will find *me* standing at the intersection of acknowledgment and understanding. Travel wisely. Think slowly. And above all else, spend some devoted time on the path to re-learning how to love the most challenging person you'll ever meet—*you*. Don't allow yourself to be defeated by your pain. You are closer than you even realize to the most powerful love you will ever know.

Yours truly,
The Truth

Dear Chosen One,

*For*give me for not having the *fore*thought to write this note *be*fore today. I have been somewhat *pre*occupied with *de*limiting my *caco*phonic life into an *im*peccable spreadsheet of precepts and formulas as a means to excel. Now complete, easy to reference, and *dis*tastefully thorough, this completed matrix of experiences even includes columns labeled for *mis*~under~standings, *over*reactions, *post*ponements, and *sub*stitutions with *cor*responding rows that detail, the previously *un*known, monthly totals, averages, and standard deviations of these semi-often interruptions in my life. Now I can methodically monitor my moments of weakness and *en*sure that my rate of emotional instability declines *dis*proportionately in relation to the rise of my sanity. Thanks to my new process of documentation, my life *trans*actions—once *ex*temporaneous sets of call and response—are now *super*structures of analyzed and deliberate *inter*communication. My life has been re-engineered to *pre*fix every thought *be*fore it *be*comes an *un*necessary *re*action.

Again, please forgive me for previous*ly* not be*ing* able to prompt*ly* respond to you in a tru*ly* person*al* way. But do know that now that I am fully upgrad*ed* and emotional*ly* efficient; I am happ*y* to answer your questions as well as steer you safe*ly* through the process of becom*ing* more comfort*able* with the answers. As it stands, you are definite*ly* my top priority and I am ready, willing, and, most important*ly*, able, to provide conscient*ious* and care*ful* promise to listen to your comments, questions, and concerns. I know that it will be hard for you to initial*ly* believe and perhaps trust me when I say "I will be there," but I hope you can different*iate* the old from the new*ly* construct*ed* me. I am commit*ting* to you in the tru*est* spirit of love and recognize that it is my purpose to remain unconditional*ly* devot*ed* to add*ing* a suffix of happi*ness* to all of your pain.

I had to learn the hard way that each word I spoke was but a letter or two from the edge of a full change in its gist. I now know that, like base words, life can be simple when I fight the urge to affix.

Best Regards,
Magical Negro

CHAPTER THREE

Creature of Bad Habits

Dear Nice Guy,

Thanks for telling me I have nice eyes, for the lovely flowers on Valentine's Day, and for the homemade CD with 13 love songs that remind *you* of me, but you're really *not* my type. You were the best when you looked after my place while I was "vacationing" with friends, for giving me lunch money during that short time (three months) when I was broke, and for sending my mom a card on her birthday. But cutie pie, I *think* we met each other at the wrong time. I am so grateful for your help with painting my bedroom, assembling my furniture from Ikea while I was at work, and for doing my laundry when I was sick. Yet sweetie, I'm just not looking for a relationship right now. Thanks for listening to me vent, laughing at all my jokes, having dinner ready when I got home, and introducing me to your family. But sweetheart, *unfortunately*, I think we're better off as friends. I remember like yesterday how you framed that picture of us, called me "baby-boy" after every other breath, bought me that sexy and expensive designer T-shirt, always asked for a kiss before you started the day, and you definitely shocked me when you wanted to break up with your man because of what "we" could have had differently. But doll face, it pains me to say, Stevie *isn't* singing *You* and *I*.

Why couldn't the fact that I trusted you mean so much more? Why couldn't the fact that you believed in me change your status as a bore? What were you thinking when you called me every night? Why in the hell did you agree to take me to the airport to catch a 5 a.m. flight? Didn't your friends tell you not to give too much too soon? What did it feel like when I told you over and over it was too damn hot to spoon? Why didn't you walk away when I was adamant about you not meeting my ex? How in the hell did you sleep in the same bed with me the past eight weeks without getting any sex? Was it worth it when you saw his hand on my ass? Did you honestly believe me when I said we were only friends and your suspicions would pass? What did your friend say when he saw me on my secret date? Did he tell you how I wasn't bothered, acknowledged him, and continued to enjoy the food on my plate? See, baby, the problem is: I need a little something extra, something exciting that you, well, just can't give.

I need you to call me at 4 p.m., hang up when I answer, and then turn your phone off until the next day. I want you to tell me how much you love me then forget my birthday and Valentine's Day within the same year. I need you to master the art of describing what your ex "use to do" in bed so that I can pretend like I like it. I want you to leave my apartment after an intense argument because you'd "rather be at home" than deal with the tension. I need you to pretend to call me at work just to hear my voice and then tell me you "have to change" our plans? I'd be so much happier if you'd invite me out to dinner and when the bill comes, matter of wackly tell me that you "prefer to go *dutch*" but you'll "get it" because my birthday is coming up. And honestly, I really do admire a man who will allow me to make him passionately scream my name and then in turn ask me for "gas money" so that he can take me home.

I'd love it if you would be so kind as to tell me you really don't like protected sex and then after five months of getting your way let me know *all* about your "commitment issues." It would *Monster's Ball* "make-me-feel-good" if you'd take your phone with you as you journey from one room to the next so you could promptly retrieve text messages from your "friends." And I'd certainly prefer that you never answer any of my questions without making me feel like I am a complete idiot for wanting to ask.

While we are arguing, tell me I'm stupid and forget to insert the being. Don't dare apologize when I find out what really happened that unfaithful evening. Screw me like a nail but bolt when I try to kiss. When I'm complaining, choose the right moment to tell me I'm acting like a bitch. Remind me that my cake from scratch is tasty but not as good as your mother's. Let me overhear you referring to me as your girlfriend because you and your brother haven't come out to one another. Lie and say you waited for five minutes and that I just didn't hear you honking your car horn. Avoid our intimacy issues by spending more time with your collection of porn. Never ever offer to wash the dishes. Tell me it's my fault that you have to go outside our relationship to scratch your other itches. Be not weary or sad if I threaten to leave. Know that joy will come in the morning even if, in your heart of hearts, you believe that God didn't intend for Adam and Steve. Only tell me you love me when you are drunk or high. And never ever give me a straight answer when I ask you why.

So cutie pie, sweetie, sweetheart, and doll face: I really do wish you weren't so nice. You remind me of the guy I used to be. You might try being more like the guy I have become.

Sincerely,
Bitter

Dear **No Strings** Attached,

Recently out of a relationship,
not looking for anything serious.
Just prefer black men in bed,
don't think there could be anything, real, between us.

See you after I hang out with my friends,
I'll come over when I'm high.
I had a bad day at work,
make me scream "don't stop" followed by "ahy"

Five foot nine, 185 pounds, in a committed relationship,
only **N.S.A.**
Can host or travel, no preference as top or bottom,
I love it either way.

Lack of commonality, musical free style,
and anesthetized emotion.
Self-Imprisonment, euphoric stupidity, unchanging pain
disguised as the right notion

After an intense mental rewind, I am completely unable to specify the decade, season, day, or the hour that we were introduced. I want to say that we met during the 2000s; however, my gut tells me it was much, much, much earlier—had to be sometime after high school during the years I *admit* to losing my gay-ginity. I *want* to say that we met in the summer, but unfortunately, it was probably just hot inside me. Must have been around the time my cloudy judgment caused my hormones to rain. I *want* to say that Molotov introduced us on a Friday because I didn't have to work the next day, yet truthfully speaking, I know that she and I often had cocktails on other days of the week so it had to be after Sunday. I *want* to say we met at midnight, but I think that was actually the hour I got sick of "loving myself." Must have been right after I got out of the shower. With all of my fuzzy "*want* to say" and approximations of "had to be," I can't begin to explain the reason why we continue to pluck each other so senselessly.

Although, I can't remember the details of when or why, I sometimes gently strum my memories to hear the impossible melodies we attempted to create. There were the numerous times I placed your shallow shoulders between my legs as you unsuccessfully—and might I add painfully—tried to make my endpin lose its balance. Before or after that, there were a few times where I held you on the left side of my jaw and desperately rotated your tuning pegs to get the G-string to sound. Then there was the time we ran out of resin and I painfully allowed you to bow octaves that should not be heard. A little before that there was a time when you decided to bring an amplifier but went into shock when the noise played too loudly in your head. And in the middle of it all, there was the time I spent not realizing that—without those four required strings—*we* couldn't produce any notes in harmony.

I know we don't talk a lot
because that's not a part of the rules
Come in, take your clothes off, lay down,
pretend it's whom you really want, see you soon

However, time has passed
and some memories are no longer present-day cute
The moment called now wants music with strings
and an entire section of jazz flute

It's time to play songs that groove to life's vibrato
and get inebriated off of common sense.
Arranged by my heart and conducted by my brain
the exact way in which it was meant

Sincerely,
High Strung

Dear If Only You Knew,

What a difference a day makes. Less than a week ago I stormed off the set of my eight-month soap opera entitled *Young and Screwless*, hopped in my Italian boots and headed straight to Bitter Bitch Day Spa for some meaningless sex and new-age facials. In true getting-over-him as well as preparatory-cleansing-for-the-next-sorry-ass-bastard fashion, I resolidified prior knowledge that all men (see letter to *"You Said You Loved Me"*)—excluding god's gift to the gays (moi)—are trifling and confused, self-absorbed, mutated puppies. Not so much the mangled should-have-been-smothered-at-birth critter, but more like a four-legged ass-licker raised by a philanthropic tribe of elephants. You see, his perceived sense of importance is as big as his stepfather's genitalia, yet he hasn't *quite* taken the opportunity to take a good look in the mirror. But then, out of nowhere and immediately following a few post-differences and articulations of "I hate men" later, I met the incredible and edible perfectly arranged caramel-covered strawberry affectionately known as YOU.

Pastor always said, "If you can't ask GOD for it, YOU don't NEED it!" And being the Christian that *I* am, I am completely convinced that my desire to drop down to my knees when I see you not only means that I need you but it also symbolizes the prophesy of our yoked love. When I was introduced to you and your man I just knew that you were the one. The way my mind transitioned to your grown-ass-man breakup, with his not-as-good-as-me self, I was confident that you were, indeed, the tattoo I always wanted and wouldn't mind having sweetly planted on my ass, arm, thigh, neck, and stomach for years to come.

I imagined that you would start by explaining to your undeserving lover how a minute in an unhappy gay relationship is far longer than normal and that based on all accepted rules of gay-dom, it was time for you to begin a more meaningful committed relationship. This time, however, with an even younger and of course more attractive man—who only *temporarily* lives 2,000 miles away. Yes, my sexy paramour, you would tell him how I dropped to my knees and how we conjured the unholy ghost while untying our tongues to an ethereal melody of randomized praise. And then you would delicately conclude by informing him that he had two-weeks-to-get-all-of-his-scattered excrement (and the damn dog) out of the house so that you could begin repainting and removing any remnants of his no-longer-important love from our new passion shack.

Next, I would send out a fierce going-to-be-with-my-new-sugar-daddy e-vite invitation to family, friends and sorry-ass ex-lovers who didn't do me right. It would say: *"Dear Friends, I have truly been blessed to meet the man that I have desperately been searching for. Join me for a night of rubbing my good fortune (and my new man) all up in your lonely single-ass-faces!"* Once the majority (primary homos that I wanted to stick it to) arrived and all were happily enjoying the heart-shaped red-velvet cupcakes with the specially ordered barbecue ribs and chicken (in honor of my journey to the Lone Star state), I would tell the DJ to play "The Sweetest Thing" from the *Love Jones* soundtrack, so that you and I could paint the room green. I would carefully caress your masculine face in one hand while coyly winking at my good-for-nothing judies as they feigned their belief in our love and commitment. For a greasy electric slide into the land of no-gay return, I would turn off the music and turn up the lights at exactly five-minutes-to-midnight to toast the beauty of a new love and being open to finding love in somebody else's man (fall back Iyanla).

Once we arrived at your house (dander and ex-man free), I would passive aggressively force you to call your job and inform them of a family emergency. After confirming your *paid* time off, I would then inform you of a surprise vacation that I had planned. Subsequent to several hours of pleading and neck-kiss-begging, I would finally concede to show you our vacation destination that only required you to pack a few bottles of Kombucha tea and Viagra. I'd whisper some semigutter sweet nothings in your ear and then proceed to take you to the international city of (Dutch accent) Dropeetlykizhaut! We would spend seven nights and zero days, making you want to slap the taste out of your parents' mouths for not teaching you that making love (nasty, sweaty, stank, slap-me, punch-me, spit-on-it, come-for-me-pa sex) could ever be this good. After six months of intense hedonism, we go to the doctor and learn that I am eight months pregnant (don't worry about the math, it's yours). You turn to me with those mature and omnipotent eyes to tell me that this just further proves that our love was meant to be. Especially, since GAWD blessed us to be the first *successful* man-on-man-breeding-team in the history of nonancient Greek civilization.

I will wrap up this letter by promising you two things: (1) You would never be unhappy because of a lack of attraction on my part! (Even though I was born the year you graduated from eight grade, I will always find you more attractive than any other piece of forbidden fruit in our local grocery store commonly referred to as New York Sports Club.) (2) You would always know where I was! (After being on Oprah with the baby, "little Magnum," the paparazzi won't leave us alone. Plus at night all you'd have to do is shine the gay bat signal and I'd hop on my swifter (for hardwood as well as tiles) and be home as quick as you can say, "Let no man tear asunder").

So baby, now that you have received this good news, aren't you excited about our impending relationship? You will be the first man who ever really knew what he wanted before he got it! Just think my love, If only-you-knew then what-you-know-now!

Sincerely,
Self-Indulgent

Dear Too Bad It Don't Pay the Bills,

So I know I'm not supposed to kiss and tell, but I just HAD to call all ten of my closest friends (who often have better and more frequent sexual encounters) and tell them "what had happened" to me last night. By the way chulo, just in case you run into one of them, please be mindful that they all hate/love you. But don't be scared Pa, it's not the same as the type of hate/love that makes you strap a bomb to your chest and walk away from the land of the living. Rather, it's the type of oxymoronic sentiment that keeps you in love with someone who is inside somebody else. It is that popular scent of right/wrong that wafts through the air amidst the untimely aromatic releases of seduction/entrapment, magnetism/desperation, and the most pungent contradiction of them all jealousy/couldn't care less. Simply stated, my friends are just not that used to me indulging in such extreme wanton pleasure. It's all good though—a good story is only as good as the next better story—and with my friends, our night of debauchery won't even make it into this year's Top 10.

Nevertheless, I remember *how* you walked up the steps of my brownstone with your cell phone pressed against your right ear while you tugged on the crotch of your slightly baggy pants with your left hand—all in an effort to show me what a burden/gift it was to be you. *How* you hugged me tightly after I closed the door and squeezed my butt/back as soon as I tried to end our embrace. *How* you came (not yet) inside my house and after shamelessly placing your jacket on the radiator, pulled out a blunt and asked, "Do/Would you mind?" *How* you puffed your herb in the shadows produced by the television while I placed my lightly oiled and semisweet smelling body half on my stomach/side, all the while pretending to be "Oh so tired" because you took so long to get here. *How* you finished your last inhalation with "damn, this shit is strong" and then proceeded to shed article after article of clothing, except for your socks and those loose/fitted, striped Gap boxers as I tried to appear refocused on what Oprah was ministering about in the repeat of the show that aired six hours earlier. *How* you then walked over to my side of the bed, squeezed my bottom lip with your index finger and thumb, and sensually asked "Whassup?" *How* with your fingers still touching my mouth I licked my lips and said, "Get in the bed." *How* you then chuckled/moaned while gently prying just enough space in/between my legs so that I would turn from my side onto my back; placed your body firmly on top of me, and with our eyes mutually locked in pre-battle stare, introduced your magic/spell to my talisman/desire and we began the wizardry that would awaken the spirits of the homo-coitus realm from their slumber.

When your tongue met my lips I felt like this moment needed/wanted music so I left our work in progress to press play on the CD player. *When* Sade started to sing "Cherish the Day," your tongue fluttered/stroked the hidden hairs of my thigh. *When* you got up to get some water because "I get thirsty when I'm high," I followed you into the kitchen and rubbed my stubble against the small/large of your back as you drank the power/courage you needed to do what you came to do. *When* you placed the glass down on the counter, I heard this little voice say, "Go for it" for which I responded by climbing on top and extending each lower extremity from one end of the counter to the other so that you might have a proper inspection/taste of the sweetest taboo coming up next.

Why you decided to scrape your teeth against my scalp and the back of my neck after you cleansed all the scented oil off—I will never/forever know. *Why* you decided to rub your entire arm repeatedly along the hairy path of my vulnerability and then proceeded to wickedly savor that same extremity in every place that had not gotten lost on your journey—somebody should/could have seen. *Why* I found that spot on both sides of your back to lightly scratch exactly at the moment when I knew I should—makes me think last night was enchanted. *Why* you were so amazed at the flavor/moistness located at the entrance to your freedom—still excites me. *Why* it was "all about you pa" or the reason you started to teach me Spanish by touch/taste is certainly not the only reason that I continue to appreciate the value of *hablando otro idioma*.

What had happened during those three hours it took me to release was what I had always/never wanted. *What* you introduced/reminded me of was the importance of advance frolic. *What* I showed/proved to you was how to nibble instead of bite while gliding/plunging your way to the top. What puzzles/informs me about you is the fact that I question what you would be like with some/none more years of experience in the bedroom. *What* is so amazing/alluring about all of this is that I know that I will/never know.

Where I learned to be an avid equestrian, I don't/won't quite remember. *Where* in the quadrant of my bed you finally decided to climax will always be outshadowed by the position. *Where* we found time to make such a deep connection in our grand total of 20 hours of being around each other is a hypothetical/whimsical question that doesn't really need to be answered. *Where* your body learned to have a conversation/debate the way that it did is truly worth discussing. *Where* we will meet/sleep the next time we come together will not depend on whether you send me flowers.

What will/should keep me from ensuring that no matter *When* you call/text me I refuse/try really hard to ignore your attempts to meet me *Where* my mind and body disconnect will rely on my realization in progress of *Why/How* the experience we just created with one another unfortunately can't pay the bills.

Best Regards,
Virgo Lover

Dear Still Addicted,

I finally received a Serenity Grant. And let me tell you, the application process was a real trip. First I had to download a three-page bubble test from the slowest Internet Web site ever made (www.iammeiamokay.com). Next, with a #2 pencil, I had to fill those empty spaces with answers to some of the hardest multiple-choice questions I'd ever seen. I would tell you what they were but the higher-ups at the Serenity Foundation have an acceptance sub-clause that states that you have to allow others to find and successfully complete applications on their own.

Anyway, once I completed the test, I had to take it to the post office where the clerk ran it through the bubble sheet scanner to see how well I did. It's okay to be wrong about yourself 5 percent of the time, so if you answer 95 percent of the questions right, you'll pass and receive a stamp on the test that says "CLOSER THAN YOU THINK." Next, I had to take the test to Serenity's local office at the Center for Inner Truth, which is located on 168th Street between Know Better and Do Better Avenues. Once there, I signed in with the receptionist, took a number and a seat. Applications are seen in the order in which your psyche has acknowledged them.

After about three months, my number appeared on the screen and I was finally greeted by Myself. Myself reviewed the application, made a few snide comments on my file and then wrote a prescription for two 5,000 mg pills of patience. After taking the pills, it took about a week for the serenity to fully kick in. And trust me, I know it sounds like a bit of work, but it's really not that bad when you consider how much easier it is to learn the courage to change the things you *can* once you have the serenity to accept the things you cannot.

Now to give you a little background, the main reason I submitted my application for the Serenity Grant was due to an unexpected addiction to three truly awful things. In no particular order, they were: Pastries, Popeyes chicken, and Dick. Eventually, I became so out of control that I had to have all three to get through my day. But on one cold day in February,

I hit rock bottom (pun intended) and it was truly the day that changed my life for the better.

For about six months leading up to February, I had developed a habit of eating these sinful chocolate chip croissants for breakfast that were sold at a newly opened coffee shop near my apartment. Now I'm not a big consumer of coffee but I decided to go in one day and get something *just* to show support for somebody who wasn't selling $5 crack in a cup. So I'm looking around the brand-new glass case with muffins, minicakes, and sandwiches and noticed a really fun yellow and red sign that says, "Try me" and there was an arrow pointing to a tray of the most beautifully golden chocolate chip croissants you could ever imagine. And even better they were only $1.50. So I bought one and after eating the first bite, I remember feeling a good wet sensation in my pelvic area followed by dizziness and weakness in my knees. Yes, I actually came. I was instantly addicted and without hesitation I confirmed the croissant as a part of my daily routine regardless of how late I was running for work.

Well, this was all good until about four months before February when they opened up a Popeyes down the street from my job. I had known about my problem with Popeyes for years, so I knew I had to be careful. However, the croissants were like weed and provided the gateway for an easy dive into my obsession with Cajun fried chicken. On the first Friday after the Popeyes opened, my office mates decided to take up a collection to get a few boxes of chicken and sides. Like a good team player, I decided to throw my $4 into the fund for clogged arteries and heart disease. I thought to myself, "A few pieces of chicken wont hurt," but boy was I wrong. I distinctly remember being on the phone when all of a sudden my nostrils were attacked by this waft of perfectly battered, seasoned, and deep fried chicken. I got off the phone with whomever I was talking with (the chicken erased my memory) and I proceeded to the conference room where I saw the familiar remains of dead chickens that had brought me so much joy.

I walked up to the box, politely placed a large leg, a crispy golden wing, and a fat, juicy breast with extra skin hanging off of it onto my plate. I then added a small serving of cole slaw and a slightly larger serving of dirty rice. Finally, I completed my lunch plate with a perfectly salt-buttered biscuit along with a packet of strawberry jam. As to really enjoy my lunch and not be bothered by the proper way to eat in front of work peers, I headed back to my cubicle where I swallowed my food (plate included) in about one minute flat. Later on in the day I coughed up the bones. And from that moment on, I had a chocolate croissant, Popeyes chicken, and a mild stroke every single day.

About two months before February, I was in line at Popeye's during my lunch break when I found myself standing next to this slim man as we both waited to order chicken. After ordering and picking up my food, I sat down in the restaurant at one of the cleaner tables and began to devour my chicken, and now, two biscuits. My neighbor from the chicken line sits at the table across from me and in a thick Trinidadian accent says, "Damn boy, you really know how to clean a bone." As I wiped the jelly from the side of my mouth with the back of my hand, I smiled and just gave him the black man's "heads-up" acknowledgement. Refusing to see that I was trying to ignore him, this bold bastard actually gets up and sits at my table and says, "What dat chicken do to you that I can."

A little taken aback, I chuckled and said, "What?" And then he responded, "Damn, ya make me wish I was born into the world with feathers!" Rude as it was, he made laugh and all I remember was that he asked to see my cell phone and added his number under the name "Dick" into my contact list. Later that night, Dick came to my house. And can you keep a secret? (I hope so) Would you believe that Dick brought me some Popeyes so he could see me clean the bone again? From that moment forward, my life was filled with chocolate croissants, Popeyes chicken, Dick, and a supersized smile on my face. I was a gluttonous mess.

Now as you can imagine, gluttony like this always comes with a price. During one of the coldest days in February and as the bill had finally been placed on the table, I was rushed to the hospital due to severe stomach pains. After doping me up with several pain relievers, the doctor, surrounded by six or seven resident nurses, told me that I contracted some rare STD that eats away at the lining of your stomach and doesn't allow you to properly digest food. Apparently, the lining of the stomach creates digestive enzymes that help break down your food and if those enzymes aren't being produced it's essentially like just placing garbage in a bag and not ever taking it out of your house. My house was full of some serious shit and—after several stomach pumps and shots of penicillin—I quickly recognized that there was something wrong with me. From the moment forward, I knew I didn't need to "almost die" before I realized that flour, chicken, and Dick (of all things) were trying to kill me!

So as a Serenity Grant recipient, I have accepted the fact that I am an addict and have gained the courage to replace chocolate-chip croissants with oatmeal and Popeyes chicken with tuna fish. And as far as Dick goes, he still comes over with Popeyes but now I'm the one who watches him clean the bone. You see, life is about balance, and I truly have earned the wisdom to know what I can change and what I cannot. It's like the great philosopher once said, "For every ailment under the sun there is a remedy, or there is none; If there be one, try to find it; If there be none, never mind it." I can give up bad food, but Dick, what would a man be without a Dick?

Prayerfully,
A Little Lighter in Mind

CHAPTER FOUR

Haughty Traveler

Dear Young Musician,

The A train seems to be your favorite place to resound. I often listen to your cadence-somewhere between mezzo forte and fortissimo with a few marcato *niggahs, fucks, shits, bitches,* and, of course, the repetition of legato *hellnall's*. With such a harmonic blend of slang and abusive language, how much attention you've been allowed to divert away from your education and a savings account toward the selection of the perfect oversized T-shirt, double-laced sneaker, ridiculously expensive jeans, and, of course, that oxymoronic hat you've labeled a "fitted" does somehow amaze me. At one of the most interesting venues in the world, you proudly show your pearly whites like the coonicatures of yesterday all the while inciting your audience to an eerily slow handclap of disgust.

Occasionally, I feel empathy or even admiration as you recite poetry, back flip, play drums, and/or sing followed by the all-too-familiar spare any change solicitation. In 90 seconds or less, you remind me of how much time you spend rehearsing for other people's money in your misguided practice of life. I know somebody told you that practice makes perfect but unfortunately, young musician, they lied with a knife. Practice makes permanent and permanent—scars, damage, and pain—isn't close to what the world really needs in its veins. I do admire your hustle and your need to make ends meet. I just don't understand why I never see your Caucasian brothers in the struggle—jumping, singing, and spinning—while I sit in my comfortable A train seat. I'm not an elitist, I was born just a little too gay and Black for that. But I do sometimes wonder during my daily commute, Why are you the only one crooning for coins over this here transit track?

Unbeknownst to you, the staccato renderings of the disparities between you and your white counterparts have finally become a full-fledged score of dark humor: *42 percent of all African-American boys have failed an entire grade at least once...More Black men earn their high-school equivalency*

diplomas in prison each year than graduate from college...The
college graduation rate for Black men is 36 percent...Black men
ages 14 to 24 are implicated in a quarter of the nation's homicides
and account for 15 percent of the homicide victims...Suicide is
the third leading cause of death among Black males...Black men
are nine times as likely as white men to die from AIDS...Life
expectancy for Black men is 69.2 years—more than six years
shorter than that of white men...Black males represent 6 percent
of the total population but comprise 40 percent of the prison
*population...*and right at the top of the crescendo...*At the*
current rate, by 2020, there will be more African-American men
in prison than there ever were in slavery.

Performed mainly by scholars, politicians, and the rest of the
world's so-called problem solvers, these lullabies somehow find
themselves murmured one right turn and seven red lights away
from the cradles of change. After a few high-pitched vamps of
role model, family, and *we*—this painful collection of jazz ends
with a fermata of hope and a decrescendo of determination.

Blame is such a powerful distraction when your reflection
does all the talking. Would your ancestors have ever made way
if they waited for their oppressors to do all the walking? To be
clear, you can "fuck bitches," "make money," and "have enough
ice to skate on a niggah" or any other colloquialism that
makes you nod your head. Just make sure you can exemplify
the great duality of our people while you scream "I'm Black
and I'm Proud," sway to "The Makings of You," and mourn,
now that "The King of Love is Dead."

You might find it interesting to know that at-risk species
are either vulnerable because of low or declining numbers,
threatened due to serious problems that need to be resolved,
or endangered due to a need for protection in order to survive.
Scientists a few years ago had the bright idea of trying to save
these animals through direct communication. So they learned a
variety of growls, clicks, coos, and even high-frequency moans
in order to warn their feeble friends of their pending extinction.

They learned that no matter how well they imitated their language or recreated their rhythms, these animals just didn't respond. As such, these scientists listened to the swan songs of nearly 750 species. Maybe, anthropologists will get together and record a few hip-hop CDs before we become 751.

Yours Truly,
No. 1 Fan

Dear Diary,

Last night, after eating that turkey cheeseburger with banana peppers and French fries from Dallas BBQ, I had the strangest dream. I was walking down the street wearing a pair of my favorite pointy-gay-mafia shoes (the ones I bought during last year's depression-shopping marathon) on what was clearly a late summer or early fall night. I was somewhat dressed up, styling a fitted pair of dark-blue boot-cut jeans, a cuffed, white dress shirt, black knot cuff links, a shiny, black tuxedo jacket as well as the power combination of sunless tanner and MAC strobe cream. Not sure why I was so dolled-up, but my guess is that I was coming from a real party and decided to push the night at little further. As you know, my dreams are always shy just short of giving me what's needed to make total sense.

At any rate, I could tell I was feeling like I was the temperature of the sun because I was giving the block my legendary supermodel walk. Remember it's the walk I created for moments when I'm extra sexy and can actually, well, mentally, transform my physical surroundings into a John Galliano show in Paris, *only* making eye contact with the zoo of photographers in front of me. I imagined myself serving the people one fierce (*feeyas*) helping of "*because I'm worth it*" and "*don't hate me cause you ain't me*" stroll as I walked down a catwalk painted blood red while Janet Jackson's "Don't Stop" is blasting through the air. I finally reached the club and entered using the notorious gay slow-motion walk from the door to the bar. I ordered a Tanqueray and tonic from the bartender and proceeded to find my spot: the place where I could scan any potential dates as they entered while totally looking like I couldn't care less. Thirty minutes and four completed cocktails later with the half-empty fifth drink in hand—*buy one get one free* special or at least that's the story I'm going to stick to— potential husband No. 148 approaches me and asks, "Can I taste it?"

Now keep in mind, I was halfway wasted but still feeling like the hottest thing since flavored vodka, so I double blinked and responded, "Taste what?" As if he had just written and published the guide to turn me the hell on, he leans in, takes a sensual deep breath as he rubs his nose against my neck and whispers in my ear, "You." I didn't respond. I finished the last of my drink, placed the glass on a table, and then gently grabbed his hand and escorted him to the dance floor. Being the liberated supermodel/ burlesque dancer I felt I was at that moment, I decided to turn my back to him and delicately place the back of my head on his chest, sliding my thumbs in his pants pocket while intricately moving my hips and other special body parts against his reason for living that night. At one point, when apparently my performance became a little too much for him to deal with, he said, "I'm starving, come home with me." I smiled and now it was him who escorted me to the next stop on our foreplay tour.

We arrive at the subway station and barely escape the closing doors of the departing D train. Outside of the lust fogs and hormone chants that were blurring the inside of the club, I am pleasantly surprised that my new friend is actually quite handsome. And as I started to ask him the last of my standard, diagnostic questions that lead to one's being labeled as a sociopath, he began to kiss me. Luckily, there was only a sleeping homeless woman on the train, but the feeling of doing something *you know you ain't got no business doing* was beyond exhilarating. He stopped kissing me abruptly and then dragged me to the end of the train car where we exited and stood on the tiny area where you are allowed to move from one car to the next while the train is moving. As we stood there, he kissed and touched me everywhere while the up-tempo version of "One Night Only" flooded my senses. Then suddenly, the train jerked and I became scared so I told him we should go back inside the car. He said, "Don't be scared, I'm not going to let anything happen to you"; and for some reason, at that moment, I totally believed him. We continued to make out until I realized that the train was now going way too fast and our bodies were violently being moved between the metal ropes connecting the two cars. So I turned around and attempted to re-enter the train car but the door wouldn't open.

At this point, in total *pulled-over-by-the-LA-police* panic, I tell him to try the other door to which he says, "Don't be scared, I'm not going too let anything bad happen to you." So I yelled at him, "Open the fucking door" and without saying a word he moves to the side as if to say, *try it for yourself.* After several pulls, I realized that we were stuck and I began to feel like I was riding a roller-coaster without a buckle or harness to protect me. The ride had mutated from the high-speed anticipatory thrills of *getting,* to the unanticipated possibility of being *shaken,* off. Oddly enough, the Kevorkian protégé who was my companion on this—the unplanned trip to my demise—seemed to be unbothered by the whole experience. In fact, he was still trying to frolic amidst the chaos and fear spewing from my pores. Annoyed, scared, and completely sober at this point, I asked him, "What the hell is wrong with you?" He calmly and somewhat cheerfully responded, "Nothing at all." I remember thinking, *Damn, how will they explain to my mother that I died trying to be a freak in between train cars?*

And then as the train prepared for what felt like an escape from the Earth's atmosphere, we were no longer underground but on an elevated train track. The train seemed to be going even faster now that the air was colder and the closest thing to my right or left side was the ground—1,000 feet below me. Holding on to my sanity and my life all at the same time, Mr. Wonderful begins to laugh hysterically; and not just the nervous kind of laugh that would be appropriate but an I'm-enjoying-the-hell-out-of-this/spin-me-again-daddy type of laugh. Now in complete shock, my tears are so heavy that it's as if I am watching and experiencing the world in a fish bowl. Overcome with fear, my knees give out and I am now forced to hold on to the chains from an undignified thunderbolt pose. Mr. Wonderful finally stops laughing, bends down, and gently raises my chin with the palm of his hand. Because I was crying so hard, I couldn't really see his face but I distinctly remember him yelling, "You were delicious," right before he maniacally jumped off the train. Two seconds later, I woke up shaking.

So Diary, as crazy as that dream was, I am writing this because I have had insomnia over the past three days thinking about what his answer to my fourth question would have been. I desperately want to start the dream all over again just to hear him respond to "What is the hardest part about being you?"

Sincerely,
Ex-Fan of Banana Peppers

PS
When he said he wasn't going to let anything bad happen to me, why do you think I believed him?

Dear Police Officer,

First of all, Napoleon, I am pissed that after making me sit in this nasty cell (without the mandatory hot prison trade) for the last six hours, you have the audacity to ask me to provide a "written statement." A written statement about what? And I know you thought you were cute when you told me to "figure it out" in that distinct Brooklyn lower-middle-class oink of yours, but it wasn't. As a matter of fact, as soon as I see my lawyer, I'm going to figure out a way to have that badge—that you treasure so much—buried so far in hog shit that not even *you* will be able to find it! But so be it, if a detailed account of the events that occurred prior to my arrest is what you want, my version of the story is what you will get!

There she was, *Miss Entitlement*: five feet six with a conservatively high heel, shoulder length Barbie hair without a single strand out of place, makeup that screams, "I want people to take me seriously," a body that whispers, "I eat a cube of cheese right before I pass out," and an air that transports you to her maternal ancestor teetering slowly in a large, white rocking chair telling the *help* to "find another cube" for her lem-o-nade. And there I was: running late to the job I couldn't stand, exhausted because I tossed and turned from my anxiety all night, aching because I had no *relations* in more than a month, dead battery in my iPod, and an awfully powerful Rosa-desire to just sit down. Besides standing next to each other on that train that morning, **we had absolutely nothing in common.** We were like night and day and the D train was the moment that connected us.

There she was, *Miss Attitude*: five foot eight, wearing hot-pink Adidas sneakers that undoubtedly glow in the ghetto, $5 Jackie O glasses hiding all of her truth (or so she thought), no makeup except for the cheap orange lipstick with some ingredient that makes her mouth reflect like a new penny in sunlight, a head of supposedly red hair pulled back into a ponytail, and a *fuck-the-world* attitude that makes you wonder why her mother just didn't swallow. And there I was: got some morning lovin' from my new *only-one-for-me*, smelling good in the custom cologne he created for me, donning the shoes I couldn't imagine using to walk out of his life, and anxious for my coworkers to compliment me on how fabulous I looked that day. Besides sitting next to each other on that train that day, we had absolutely nothing in common. We were like heaven and hell, and the A train was the thought that connected us.

There she was, *Miss Oblivious*: five foot nine wearing truly worn-down *Mary Janes* with her ankles bulging over the sides, really short natural brown hair that shows off "such a pretty face," sweat tattooed around her forehead, a powdery scent that reminds you of a Victorian whorehouse, and two bags over each shoulder containing her Entenmann's medications used for her self-diagnosed "hypoglycemia." And there I was: been to church (the gym) every day that month, in Popeyes withdrawal, just broke up with the *one* (again), and feeling very antisocial towards anything on God's browning earth that was capable of talking back. Besides standing next to each other on that train that day, we had absolutely nothing in common. We were like Olympic Gold and Olympic Bronze, and the 1 train was the time that tied us together.

At first, everything was fine. Then as the 1 train arrived at the 125th Street station, I sighed to the tune of "Aww Hell" as I watched the angry mob of cartoonish characters push and shove their way onto this, the only train that would bring them any satisfaction. I took a deep breath, found the coziest spot to be trapped like a clothed sardine, and braced myself for my imminent mauling. So when the buckle of Miss Oblivious's Chinatown bag bumped into the right side of my rib cage, I just chalked it up to "no room to move," "she didn't mean to," "she is probably getting off at the next stop," "I need a vacation," and a few other handy self-meditations I learned to keep me from snatching a bitch. Then, as we approached the 59th Street station, I came to the realization that I had been caught in a trap containing every damn person who, like me, would only seek their freedom after six more stops. As such, I knew this bag-bumping business had to end. So I politely said, "Excuse me, your bag is bumping into me" to which she replied, "Oh, umm, I'm sorry, I didn't know." I dismissed her violation of my personal space as she slid her purse down her shoulder and placed its handle in her left hand.

Now, as my luck would have it, the damn purse had a large silver belt buckle with a rough matchstick-shaped tongue that felt like it had been sharpened to engrave cement. And as God was testing me, the tarnished tongue of her belt buckle began to prick and jab at my right leg. This time annoyed, I said, "Excuse me, your belt buckle is jamming into me." I had hoped that based on the inflection and loudness of my voice she would have moved the piece of shit bag to the other side, in front of her, or even on the floor. Hell, I really didn't care. I just wanted her to prevent the knock-off from drilling my body parts for blood. **That's when, she, who didn't know me at all, said** (half-frustrated and sincerely curious), "Well, what do you want me to do about it?"

At first, everything was fine. Then as the A train arrived at 59th Street, I sighed to the tune of "Here We Go" as I saw a group of Asian tourists (don't get me to lying about the specific nationality) eagerly lined along the platform ready to get to their next destination in Manhattan. However, as my luck would have it, two seats became available—one for me, and one for *Miss Attitude.* So, my next-seat-neighbor who was now satiated from the pleasure of taking a seat from a hard-working adult, arrogantly sat next to me with her earphones on *Stone Deaf Before Thirty.* Once we arrived at 42nd Street, the train captain announced—over an ancient PA system that made him sound like he was performing the little known circus act of gargling cotton balls with an Oreo milkshake—says "Attention passengers, Brooklyn-bound A-trains will be making all local stops." As we approached the 34th Street station, I realized that her music was giving me a headache and that's when I repeatedly tried to get her attention until she looked up from her handheld game, removed one earphone, and finally said, "What?"

Knowing who I was speaking to, I said, "Yo, your music is mad loud can you please turn it down a bit?" She didn't respond verbally. However, she physically responded by placing her earphone back in its rightful place and by increasing the volume to *Aliens Can Hear This.* I looked around for another seat but there wasn't one. My eyes did, however, stumble across a sleepy toddler lying on his mother's side with his right hand covering his ear. He and I desperately wanted her unsolicited concert to end and that's when I decided that enough was enough. I assumed that she was young enough to respect me in the way that normal teenagers respected adults. So, again, I said excuse me while waiving my hand in front of her to get her attention. She yanked both earphones out and asked, "What the fuck?" In my most adult and James Earl Jones-like voice I said, "Watch your mouth. You are disturbing everybody on this train who paid their money just like you did. You need to turn your music down." That's when, she, who didn't know me at all, said (defiant and fearless), "And if I don't. Well, what you gonna do about it?"

At first, everything was fine. Then as the D train arrived at the West 4th Street station, I started singing "Oh Happy Day" as the elderly man in the seat right in front of me prepared to exit the train. So I gave him enough room to leave and slid comfortably in my long-awaited seat. Then suddenly, I see this doll-like finger bounce three times on my knee. I look up and see Miss Entitlement, who was noticeably outraged and said, "It would be nice if you would let me sit down." A little taken aback, I looked over her frame to make sure she wasn't pregnant or elderly, then responded, "Yes, it would." She then says, "Why don't you be a man and let me sit down?" At first I realized that that the bitch was crazy, so I did my best to ignore her. She clearly had *just* had an emotional breakdown and the evil jokester called Life decided that I was to be the unlucky mofo to receive today's gag. In the middle of trying my best to ignore her, she begins yelling at me: "It's poor excuses for men like you that make this city a horrible place to live." Trying to be calm and remembering my occasional bias against white women I said, "You need to get out of my face, lady." That's when, she, who didn't know me at all, said, (arrogantly and belligerently), "What will you do if I don't?"

And honestly, Napoleon, that's all I remember before I blacked out. I don't remember Ike-slapping the shit of her like I had five hands, snatching the earphones out of her ear and performing a Flamenco routine on her iPod like I was possessed; nor do I remember taking her bag and repeatedly swinging it against her side like she was a piñata. And there is absolutely no way that I called her a poor white trash bitch, an unnecessary statistic, or the place where fat goes to die. I would never forgive myself for spitting on her, cussin' at her so badly that she started to cry, or taking each item out of her purse and throwing it in her face as she desperately screamed for help. Do you really think a man with an advanced education would behave in such a low manner? I don't have a criminal record and have never, ever, been accused of anything like this before. So why are you so convinced that I was the man who "lost it" on the security camera? I wouldn't...I mean I couldn't...but wait...*did* I?

Sincerely,
Might Need a Good Lawyer

Dear Hate Taking the Train,

Yesterday was really an odd day. I decided to make the trek to Century 21 to pick up a few pairs of underwear, man stockings, and other stuff on sale. Now this in itself, for anybody who knows me, is strange considering my not-so-private disdain for the store's mantra: fashion worth fighting for. Yes, indeed, this overstocked merchandise hell is replete with credit-card warriors willing to sacrifice their broken-condom offspring for 60 percent off the original price, horrific sights of cashmere sweaters on plastic hangers and nasally confrontational (politically correct term for stank-ass) tourists who choose to use the aisles as fitting rooms. And to round out this nightmare masked as a shopping experience, you are ridiculed immediately after your purchase as your receipt is loudly stapled to your bag in 10 to 15 places while America's Next Top Statistic says, "Have a nice day," as if those four words were a curse. I promise you, Century 21 most certainly deserves the award for "Most Uncivilized Shopping Experience" in Manhattan. But I digress.

Like I said, I was heading downtown to shop and once seated on the train I realized that I had done the absolute unthinkable. Just like the true genius (idiot) that I can be from time to time, I brought nothing to read, nothing to listen to, and an eerie alertness that would prevent my *I Dream of Jeannie* infused with Stevie Wonder sleep nods. So like a big baby, I had nothing to do but observe the all-too-familiar moving portraits of unknown lives going to or coming from someone, someplace, or something—just like me.

In the first few minutes, I noticed the CUNY advertisements whose "relatable" photographs of their star faculty, researchers, and students were in desperate need of digital retouching. Maybe it's just me, but I just don't understand how "city" colleges believe they will attract students by advertising images of not-so-attractive or facially offensive (politically correct term for ugly) people. Hell, everybody knows that most of us—who weren't forced to go to college—were only interested in learning whether or not the tales of binge drinking, comalike sleeping, and promiscuous sex were real. And everybody also knows that nobody wanted to develop those three bad habits in the company of anybody other than hormone-dripping, sexually uninhibited, picture-perfect men gathering around sadomasochistic swing sets and library glory holes (don't judge me). So maybe next year, they'll advertise McSteamy student athletes and McDreamy professors seductively posing like porn stars beneath a tongue-in-cheek tagline that reads, "The Stories Are True!" I think it's a no-brainer that enrollment numbers will increase. Hell, I might even go back for another degree my damn self!

Anyway, once I was bored with the CUNY ad, I saw the "Now you can have beautiful clear skin" ad that always makes me chuckle. I mean first and foremost, the "board certified dermatologist," who takes all major credit cards and works on Sundays, is named Dr. Zizmor or "Dr. Z" for short. His name sounds like that of a poorly written soft-core porn actor on the Playgirl channel. Secondly, the ridiculous before-and-after pictures looked as if "Before" was recently attacked in the face by honeybees while "After"—a completely different person altogether—had just won the Miss America Pageant. But without a doubt, the funniest part of the ad has to be Dr. Z's face. It's a hybrid between the guy who kidnaps the boy in the *I Know My Name Is Steven* movie and the star of the sitcom *Dexter*. Funny enough, I noticed that when blinking really fast while looking at Dr. Z's face, that I could make out the words "patient molester." All jokes aside, I really don't think I would trust Dr. Z to shine my shoes, let alone place chemicals on my face. But once again, I digress.

After a few other observations and moments of self-induced chuckling, I arrived at 42nd Street where this unquestionably homeless man enters the train. Now I must admit that he made me a bit uncomfortable because without my usual distractions I had nothing to help me pretend like I wasn't looking at him. His presence reminded me of my warped efforts as a kid to pretend like I was "too mature" to stare at a vertically restricted person (politically correct term for midget) or try not to look at a person with Michael Jackson syndrome (politically incorrect term for vitiligo). Each and every time I tried to look away or keep my head down, my curiosity would jerk my attention back into his direction. There was clearly some irony in how quickly I transitioned from looking for distractions to being, what felt like, distracted against my will. I had clearly been uncareful about what I had wished for during that unpredictable train ride.

After the train doors closed, the homeless guy mumbled a few undistinguishable words and carried his two large Hefty-style garbage bags in one hand towards a seat. He sat directly in the middle of a train bench where he was flanked by a woman stage right and two men stage left. I was seated directly across from them. Almost instantly following the sigh from his relief to be sitting down, he clumsily tried to spark a conversation with the woman to the left of him.

In what seemed to be a drunken and aggressive articulation, he said, "Where you headed?" She didn't respond and looked intently at her *Glamour* magazine as if it had a magical noise cancellation feature. So he asked again, only this time even louder, "Where you headed?" Noticeably aggravated, she sucked her teeth and huffed away to the other end of the train while the man stared at her back in an oddly disappointed way. Looking almost as if he wanted to say, "Don't go."

Once the woman had vanished offstage, in an almost comical manner, the homeless man scooted his body next to the first man on his right and said, "What you listening to?" Similarly annoyed, this guy didn't wait for the final syllables of the homeless man's question. He quickly gathered his entangled groceries and joined his "bench peer" in the wings of this moving impromptu performance. I could vaguely overhear their relocated chatter as they shared stories about "crazy motherfuckers" and "where's police when you need them." Then, finally, with one last potential actor to approach, the homeless guy propels himself into a body slide that finds him at the end of the bench where he accidentally (my assumption) bumps into a young white dude in his early to mid-thirties who was reading a book.

After bumping into the guy, the homeless man's face transitioned from a brief soberness that expressed "Oops" and then back into the hard-life portrait that covered his identity. This time his question, "What you reading?" unlike the others, began like the shot from a cannon and faded into a distant whimper. It was as if he thought this was his last attempt to ever get an answer from anyone about anything. At that moment, he exhibited a sense of despair that made me feel bad for him. So, as I was doing what any person who has not grown up in NYC does, I started going through my murse to find spare change. As I finished scraping the bottom of the bag, the young guy— resembling one of the people in the CUNY ads (actually not that bad in person)—turned to the homeless man and in a suburban jock-inspired voice asked, "What?"

Now smiling, the homeless man, using the three essential childlike tones for asking a question, responded with, "What you reading?" The guy answered him by showing him the front of the book, which was then followed by the homeless man asking, "It any good?" And as if I was watching some freak of nature subway moment on the History Channel, the young white guy (reminded me of those people who signed up for Peace Corps to build houses for pre-historic mosquitoes living on the South Side of Nicaragua) replied, "Yes."

After "yes," not only does he tell the homeless man that the book is "really cool" but he also begins to explain the book's title, some of the author's other works, and what the book is really all about. Now I have to tell you, I have seen a lot of things on the subway—oral sex, fights, projectile-puking white girls—but this really and truly took the cake. In no more than three minutes, these perfect strangers were in an exchange about books, about life, and about memories of words without any regard or respect for the labels that had made the moment so obviously peculiar. They ignored the past that had made one of them homeless. They ignored the future that would make it highly unlikely that they would ever speak or see one another again. They only focused on what was then, that which seemed to be the most important thing happening in their lives—their now.

As it became time for the young guy to leave the train, while still talking with the homeless man, he returned the book to its place in his bag and then stood up to quickly place each of the bags' two straps around his shoulders. After the bag was secured on his back, he briefly sat on the edge of the bench, extended his right hand to the homeless man and told him that his stop was coming up next. The homeless man embraced the young guy's hand with both of his hands and said, "Thanks, brother." And as if he knew what he was being thanked for, the guy said, "No problem, man." When the young guy left the train, the homeless man placed his Hefty bags in the space where the young guy had been sitting and then crossed his right leg over his left while folding his arms at his waist. When I looked at his face now, he looked as if he had just won something so important that he couldn't even remember fighting for it. He looked as though all in his world was the way it should be. He was the portrait of contentment.

As it became my time to leave the train, I decided to balance the act of doing a good deed with the notion of giving this man something tangible to somehow add to what was obviously gained from his recently ended conversation. As such, I extended my hand to him with two one-dollar bills folded between my thumb and index finger.

After leaving the train station, I thought about the homeless man's first question, "Where you headed?" And then I thought about the second and third questions he asked, "What you listening to?" and "What you reading?" Then I thought about James Baldwin's *Another Country*, the book they had discussed. Then I remembered the homeless man's face with picture-perfect contentment as he declined my two dollars with "I'm good brother."

I thought about the annoying questions that Life would sometimes bother me with. The questions that I would either pretend not to hear or preemptively avoid. I thought about how much time I had spent ignoring a part of myself for fear that it would one day become the whole. I thought about how I sought kindness expressed through a few unexpected dollars, when in fact, to be content all I really sought was respect. That moment spent without any of my usual distractions during that train ride has become so much more than a coincidence. It is a reminder.

Sincerely,
Left Leg Crossed Over Right With Arms Folded at My Waist

CHAPTER FIVE

Very Perceptive, Practically Psychic

Dear Soul Mate,

   I am merrily rowing my life down a stream of positive thinking and self-actualization. It seems just like yesterday that I was trapped in a watching paint-dry cycle of sexual monotony with relief nowhere in sight. Then, as fate or subconscious positive thinking would have it, I stumbled across *The Secret* and found myself a true believer in the doctrine of "Create it in your head and it will become real." As any normal homo-believer would, I decided to focus my mental energy on the visualization of a low budget and unreleased (hopefully) *sex-u-men-tary* entitled, "Me and You Two." Through much meditation, (thank you xtube.com) I willed a three-and-a-half-hour, seven-condom, half-bottle-of-good-lube, nine-tequila-shot, verge of insanity-*3some* into my life. And, as if that wasn't enough, I also lost twenty pounds (while eating all the carbs I wanted), got rid of the mice in my East Harlem garden apartment, and even received a letter from the IRS informing me I could pass on filing taxes this year because of my great nonprofit work.

   So now that those *medi-fes-tations* have been realized, the stop on this love boat, <u>Next</u>: *a hue that makes the sun proud to shine, newborn eyes that were stolen from the universe's vault of stars, a mouth that tells the story of smiles beating frowns 10:1, hair (everywhere) that knows how to be smooth and when to be rough, legs and thighs that send black stallions into a white-girl hysterical fit, hands that could be used to rebuild Jericho from scratch yet more eye catching than any diamonds they hold, a fat little pouch for a stomach that giggles at the rest of its more muscular neighbors, a verbena/musk/patchouli/clove mixed scent that makes me think of Dorothy's Home in "The Wiz," a satiating taste that transports me to fall picnics and first bites' of Gala apples, and more than enough height to reach God via tippy-toe*—<u>is You</u>.

   We will meet during the annual Gay Day festivities at Six Flags Great Adventures in September where my entourage will include "Judy No. 1" and his always-new boyfriend, "Judy No.

2" and his boyfriend that has tap-danced on my nerves for the past four years, and the ever so complicated and notoriously single, (big-time whore) Judy No. 3. Well, now that I think about it, scratch Judy No. 3 because at the last minute he will *back* out after getting drunk and repeatedly *banged* out the night before by re-visited fake "trade." Anyway, as the unscripted five of us enter the park, my facial expressions will range between "mad about it" and "distant disgust" as I take those awful group pictures that will go into the stupid-ass key chains I am always suckered into buying. After hours of strolling behind my friends and their part-time lovers (to appear like I was sexy enough to come by myself), I will excuse myself from the group and re-construct my happiness by demolishing a funnel cake layered with vanilla ice cream, caramel syrup, shaved pecans, and one cherry to represent the pinnacle of overpriced gluttony.

After sensually licking the cardboard plate, I will walk to my favorite two-seater roller-coaster, *Popper,* and strategically maneuver so that I get to sit in the front car. While standing there with my nerves bubbling over with anxiety, I will be startled by your deeply baritone voice as you say, "Excuse me, do you mind if I ride with you?" Processing your unnecessary request, I'll halfway turn my face to mumble, "Sure, no problem." You'll respond, "Thanks a lot man. One of my friends didn't show up, so now I'm third wheel to my boy and his partner." I'll think to myself, *ironic,* but my thought will get sidetracked as it becomes time to cross the metallic gates into *forty-five-second hell.* As I pull the harness over my head and into my chest, our arms will rub against each other creating a pop of electricity that is anything but static.

After the ride, we will end up standing side by side at the video kiosk, where you'll turn to me and say something corny like, "We look really good together." I'll smile as I begin to respond with something cute and dismissive but get tongue tied as I am, <u>Overwhelmed:</u> *I hide in your peace when I'm scared to be me, I trust you as far as the worst possible day can throw you, morning comes when we make it good, anger disappears with your kiss on the back of my neck, dinner is delicious because you make it home, the maze of no return is mad at you for finding my unconditional love, extra joy is squeezed onto the world when we embrace, our bodies were designed for each other to claim and explore, hearing your voice makes me forget tomorrow and remember always, the two of us are an army of Love, our kisses make God smile:* <u>by You</u>.

Once I regroup, I'll suggest that our friends meet up and continue through the park together. You'll say, "Anything to sit close to you again," and I <u>Will:</u> *welcome the part of you that is hated the most, make it better like only I am, fight for us harder than the left of the right, put the secret herb called me in every meal, use my voice to give life to more than just your fantasies, let you take, make, and stake all of my goodness as your own, give you enough room to hang yourself but never the right rope, decipher when your silence needs to be loudly heard, penetrate your brain until we come understood, help the natural boy in you love being my man:* <u>for You.</u>

We will spend the rest of the day strolling through the park, flirtatiously exchanging words and nonaccidental body brushes, until Gay Day comes to an end. To the chagrin of my now "mad about it" and "distantly disgusted" duo of Judy, you will ask me if you can give me a ride home and I will happily agree. When we arrive at my house, you will park and ask, "What is your favorite song?" And before I can say, Meshell NDegéocello's *Andromeda & the Milky Way* the alto saxophone in my heart will begin to play. We'll kiss each other good-right and moments after I find "comfortable" in my bed, you'll call to be near my voice, <u>Just</u>— *like real Love has a capitalized* ***L***, *as you and I have we*—<u>for Me.</u>

Love Always,
Dreammaker

Dear Eighth Grade Class of 2040,

Before the year 2010, the heterogeneity of African-Americans had remained harmonious, with *most* black people viewing Caucasians (known derogatorily as crackers or honkies) as the main oppressor in their lives. However, in 2009, during the month of February, which was then known as Black History Month, one event would send a discordant wave through the entire African- American community. It would incite Black-on-Black crime unlike the world had ever seen. This single moment, without question, would serve as the catalyst for the *African-American Civil War,* occurring between the years 2010 and 2016. Creating one of the most unfortunate and calamitous periods in the history of America, the day of February 14, 2009, will always be remembered as the day media mogul Queen O aka O was killed by rap artist Ten Nickels aka *Nickels.*

The Marvel's Ball held on Valentine's Day in the year 2009 was intended to be Queen O's third annual celebration of African-American women in the arts and entertainment. With media in attendance from around the world, celebrities navigated an endless red sea of press /photographers outside of Lincoln Center. Surprising all in attendance, Brown Entertainment Television aka BET, sent rap artist Nickels as a correspondent in a ploy to create media attention for the poorly watched network. At the time, he and Queen O had a highly publicized feud over her less-than-supportive comments regarding artists who chose to use degrading lyrics in their music. When the BET executive jokingly asked Nickels to be a correspondent, they were shocked at how eager he was to take the job. They knew this would make headlines, but they certainly didn't expect for events to transpire in any, way, shape or form as they did.

After O exited her limousine at approximately 7:30 p.m., she was instantly greeted by the strobe light of frenzied photographers. Almost blinded by the flashes, she slowly made her way through the paparazzi chaos when suddenly she saw Nickels in ghetto-fabulous regalia holding a microphone in one hand and his crotch in the other. It is believed that several of

O's key staff members urged her to bypass the BET crew, but O was insistent on giving them the "moment they wanted." She made her way over to the BET station; and at 7:50 p.m., she promptly told Nickels how pleased she was to see him, as well as BET, present to celebrate the night's honorees. Nickels replied, "Me too," and O, being O, sarcastically asked Nickels when was he going to "produce a clean record" so that she could have him on her show. Nickels replied, "When you're dead bitch," and he proceeded to pull out a pistol from his crotch and shoot at O three times: the first bullet grazing her shoulder, the second bullet barely missing President Uhdadi's wife, and the last determined bullet passing directly through O's heart. The President's secret service team immediately gunned down Nickels before he could fire his fourth shot. After several laborious hours of surgery, Queen O took her last breath at 10:49 p.m. One minute later, at 10:50 p.m., the world, as *most* knew it, would change forever.

On July 1, 2009, Congress passed *The Pure Ignorance Act* 99:1, which banned the possession, sale, or manufacturing of music with explicit lyrics. Offenders were punished by indefinite exile to Antarctica and/or by lynching. During Uhdadi's televised presidential address, he promoted the ban as a much-needed step in the war on ignorance. He vowed to dedicate "significant resources to stop the malicious bollworms from eating away at the fabric of society." He closed his speech with the following: "It is because of these cretinous parasites in our society that Queen O is dead and my wife was almost killed. Therefore, it is my responsibility not only as the President but also as an African-American to make sure we don't lose any more good *Black Folks* to ignorance. *Niggahs* beware!"

Immediately following the President's landmark speech, three rap artists, *Crazie, Tiny Whim, and E-Fiminute*, organized the Niggah Army. The *Niggah Army* who—in a fashion, all be it slightly similar to Spartans—were trained to be violent, fearless, and detached from the moment they were born. *Most* who were brought into the world by careless young girls and sperm-throwing boys were breast fed by McDonalds, sung lullabies by Gangsta Rappers, baby-sat by cable televisions, sent to school with low expectations, and never, ever, allowed to create an individual identity. Using secret Ebonic e-mails, underground meetings, and downloaded music over an encrypted server, they profusely spread the message of Niggah love. As a true slap in the face of the President's speech they even created a compilation CD of revolutionary songs entitled *Grimy: Niggahs for the Revolution* which encouraged party members to hold on to the Niggah way of life by the many means possible. When President Uhdadi learned of the CD, he was outraged. He called for an immediate Congressional vote to go to civil war. On January 5, 2010, Congress approved the African-American Civil War and one week later the *Army of Black Folks* was sent to every U.S. ghetto to hunt for sagging pants, unkempt cornrows, cocked baseball caps, gold teeth, cars with rims, extra-long painted fingernails, overly gaudy jewelry referred to as *bling*, persons listening to any form of Niggah music, and anybody, any age, standing on or near a street corner for longer than 3 hours.

Unfortunately, President Uhdadi did not properly account for the strength of the Niggah Army and the overwhelming apathy of the *Pawns*, folks who praised God on Sunday after they had raised hell at the club on the Saturday before, boasted to coworkers about their collection of Monk CDs without mention of the *Lil Ron* they played during their daily commute to and from work, called somebody or something "ghetto" while proudly serving every family meal on paper plates, and worked hard at keeping up with the Joneses while letting the Whites' pass them by. President Uhdadi's vision for a pest-less society created seven years of destruction where more than 6 million people of color died as *Niggahs* fighting *Black Folks* violently snatched each other from the land of the free and buried handfuls of casualties in the cemeteries of the slave. It was truly a bloody war: AME churches were bombed, strategically located fried chicken shacks were sent salmonella-marinated chickens, HBCU students attacked one another in their sleep, key members of the NAACP/UNCF/100

Black Men were seduced then murdered by the Nappy Headed Ho Intelligence Collective (NHIC), low-income housing in every major city was destroyed by beer-seeking missiles, and thousands of families were trapped on Martha's Vineyard when a group of Niggahs took over the ferries.

In 2016, after Uhdadi's second term as President, the United States elected its first openly gay president, Basil Ford. Ford, a respected Congressman, had long been against the war and in fact was the only congressman who had opposed both the Pure Ignorance Act and the African- American Civil War. So Ford, now President, consulted with Colin Cowie to throw an elaborate dinner party where he convinced the two sides to stop fighting for a period of three months while he came up with a mutually agreeable solution.

On August 24, 2016, President Ford persuaded Congress to pass the Fiercely Fair Reparations Act, which did five key things: (1) allowed all African- Americans to attend any college/ university or trade school—once accepted—for free; (2) heavily fined city mayors where acceptance rates of African- American high-school seniors by institutions of higher education was less than 90 percent; (3) made all housing expenses free for those working directly with disadvantaged African-American youth; (4) mandated arts curriculum in all inner-city public schools from K-12; and (5) provided serious tax credits and no-interest-rate housing loans for parents raising African-American students who maintained a B+ average. These five policies laid the foundation for an incredible new beginning in the African-American community.

Niggahs forgot about the Niggah Way and began to fight for their right to be educated versus their right to be ignorant. Soon, they were creating clean hip-hop and rap music through "O Happy Day Recordings," which was the first music label they founded in memory of Queen O. The Black Folks army dissolved as members removed themselves from their meaningless corporate jobs and started a variety of nonprofits in the communities they were raised. Not only working hard for their own children, Black Folks began to care about the entire African-American community. Around 2020, the Pawns vanished; they couldn't decide whether it was more important to be free or not to be, so they lynched themselves in Antarctica.

Yours truly,
Living Text Book

Dear Friend in My Head,

Wendy, *How you doin'?* A few months ago, I called the Bureau of Missing Persons and spoke with Rick, this straight man (yes, you can always tell) who was really quite rude to me. He consistently interrupted the details of my case with "huh," "who?" as well as "are you serious?" And as if finding one that you have loved and lost isn't painful enough, right after I asked if there was someone else I could speak with regarding this matter, he carelessly disregarded the pain and longing in my voice and forwarded my call to Mr. Dial Tone. Now, as I am sure that you are aware (Play Crickets), when an individual is dealing with the mental unrest that comes with searching for a missing person, it's imperative that they be treated with dignity and care. Clearly, *Splaboo* either didn't understand this or made the decision that he could dismiss my case because *I'm gay, I'm a homo. I like guys.* In either instance, it was unnecessarily insensitive so I decided to meet Rick in person to give him a piece of my mind. You see, I have anger management issues and living in NYC over the past few years, I have learned that sometimes you have to get a little extra "ethnic" on people in order to teach them a lesson. So that's why I showed up at the Bureau headquarters fully prepared to invoke my Irish ancestry. (Play *Leave It to Beaver*)

I arrived right at the time when all city workers have managed to shut down their computers, place their phone on "away," and pee one last time before they head home—4:35 (Play African bells). After a brief conversation with the security guard, I was assured that all the employees from the building exited out of the same door and therefore I knew it was only a matter of time before I would meet Rick and freely provide some tough love. Dressed as a limousine driver (a leftover outfit from a kinky sexual phase where I was into role play), I stood in the front of the building holding a bottle of champagne in one hand and a half-dozen white roses in the other hand. I wore a sign around my neck with the name RICK in red bold letters.

The first Rick that came out was some guy in accounting who flamed brighter than the grease from a hot link sausage on a summer grill. As luck would have it, I had to give him the flowers to stop him from crying after not-so-gently assuring him that his jump-off for the past six years had *not* decided to take him to Paris for his birthday weekend (Play donkey sound). Anyway, a few minutes later, I get this chill down my spine as I make eye contact with this really handsome man. He comes over to me with an ice-melting smile and says, "Are you looking for Rick Hard in Missing Persons?" After recognizing that the voice of the rude asshole on the phone was connected to this fine-ass specimen of a man, I suddenly had to seek consul with my brain.

Whenever I have a truly difficult decision to make I place the world on pause and meet with my special advisers Charlotte (aka Charlie) and Samantha (aka Sammy). So before I could even get "What should I do?" out of my inner mouth, Sammy in her aggressive and—for lack of a better word—*hood* approach, says to me, "Look fool, that bastard hung up the muthafuckin phone on us. I know good and damn well you ain't rethinking what the fuck we came here to do. So what if he is cute, you don't even know if this prick is gay and you acting like you wanna give him a *professional* or some shit. Also did you forget you are wearing this stupid-ass getup and you don't even have a car let alone a limousine? Are you seriously thinking about changing plans? You've got to be kidding me. Proceed as planned dummy. I'm done. Alright Charlie, go ahead with your fake-ass bullshit. Oh and one last thing, please remember that the last time you didn't listen to me you gained ten pounds from all of the anger your dumb ass held inside. Go head Charlie."

Now Charlie, always the polar opposite of Sammy, responded, "Just look at his smile, that smile couldn't hurt anyone or at least not cause harm on purpose. You have to be forgiving and realize that people have bad days and good days (Play Crickets) and maybe you simply caught him during a difficult moment in his life. We have to treat people with love. Although you are dressed in this limousine costume, you can always just say you are waiting for someone else and let him go on with his day. You will feel much better for doing the right thing in the morning.

Violence is never the answer. Remember, what the world needs now is…" Sammy interrupted, "Fuck that, what the world needs now, and I mean right now, ain't love, it's understanding. And the only way you gone get this silly ass man to understand that it's not right to hang up on somebody is to run up and down the back of his head with this bottle of *Cook's* and pray for heaven later. Mama didn't raise no punks. Aww hell, you know what I mean. (Momma!), didn't raise no sissies. Ok look, you know what I'm trying to say. Do what we came to do. Grab your nuts and cough, fool." Charlie tried to finish her advice, but I suddenly jumped back into real time when Rick asked, "Are you looking for me?"

Since, Sammy got the last word in, I thought it was best to follow her advice. I mean, despite her vulgar words, she was really right: It was my civic duty to teach Rick a lesson. You can't just dismiss people because you don't understand them. So, I responded to Rick, "Yes Rick, I am looking for you. You have just won an all-expense-paid trip to Miami from WGAY Radio. My limousine is parked in the alley behind the building and you don't have to worry about anything. Let's go!" You could tell Rick was one of those arrogant men who thought the world revolved around him. And honestly, why shouldn't it—he was the kind of guy who made you imagine yourself butt-naked in the middle of the woods screwing (Play Sucking Sound) like it was a scene from *Poetic Justice* or *Brokeback Mountain* (yes, the tent scene). But I have to say, when his only response to my false promise of an all-expense weekend was "That's whassup," I started to feel much better about following Sammy's advice.

As we walked down the block and turned into the alley, I started to hype myself up by asking him a bunch of questions about his day. In straight-boy speak I said, "Man, missing persons, that's gotta be a hard thing to do everyday, right?" He says, "Yeah man, especially when you get calls from crazy-ass people." And suddenly, I was holding the champagne bottle firmly by its neck. I said, "Really? (Play crow sounds) Like what kind of crazy-ass people?" He says, "Son, like today for example, this crazy-ass fag calls me and tells me he wants to file a report because he can't find a *top*. (Play explosion) Dude, I just hung up on his dumb-ass because he clearly was just some crack-head fag." (Wow, wow, wow, wow) I responded, giggling coyly, "That's pretty incredible that you would hang up on him." He said, "What do you mean?" I said, "Well, what if the fag wasn't a crack-head? What if the fag was smart enough to develop some elaborate scheme to get back at you?" He interrupted, without even thinking, "Honestly, all that fag could think about was some dick. I'm so not worried."

As we had reached the middle of the alley and he had adequately reignited the anger in me, it was at that moment that I cracked the bottle of champagne over that handsome head of his. (Play explosion) After being called a fag in third person a few times, I definitely felt justified. I took off my driver's hat, which was saturated with nervous sweat, and removed my specially purchased "loosy" from my pants pocket. I lit the cigarette and began my theatrical re-enactment of the legendary (*Alright!*) Angela Bassett puff and stroll in *Waiting to Exhale*. Only in my scene, there was an unconscious man lying next to a garbage dump instead of a burning car being left in the background.

A few days later (Hey!), I started to feel guilty. Charlie had begun to make me feel bad and no matter what Sammy said to dismiss her comments I knew that Charlie was right. So I decided to find the hospital where Rick had been admitted and visit him. Even though I had full knowledge that I would probably be arrested if he recognized me, I felt like I needed to right my wrong (Play funeral song). So when I arrived, I told the nurse that I was there to visit Rick Hard and she asked if I'm family and I kind of lied and said yes. I mean, I am, but just not the family she was talking about. She told me that Rick didn't remember much about the incident and that he was going to be ok. So I walked in and said, "I'm really sorry...," and before I could finish my sentence, in a shockingly calm state he said, "No, really its ok. This is just the wake-up call I needed." I said, "Come again?" He said, "I have been hiding who I am all of

VERY PERCEPTIVE, PRACTICALLY PSYCHIC

these years and honestly if I could meet the guy who attacked me, I'd shake his hand for reminding me that tomorrow is not promised." Confused and slightly opportunistic, I said "So you don't remember who did this to you?" He said, "It doesn't even matter. I'm just happy that from this day forward I'm not going to live a lie anymore." (Play horns) I couldn't believe the irony in all this: Rick was gay but never allowed himself to admit it.

At that point, I said, "By the way, I was looking for my uncle but I must be on the wrong floor. That's why I said I apologized when I walked in." He said, "Well I guess you got a lot more than what you bargained for then!" We both laughed. And that's when I introduced myself and said, "So did you...I'm gay and we can hang out anytime you're ready." He said, "That's Whassup. By the way, I'm Rick Hard." And as I shook his right hand, I noticed that his blanket wasn't doing a very good job of hiding his last name. I gave him my number and told him to call me if he needed anything. And to my awkward surprise, he called. Once Rick left the hospital, we met on a few occasions for dinner and drinks. We would sit and talk, and talk, and talk. And one day, after drinking way too much *Crown Royal on Ice*, mutually flirtatious conversation led us back to his place where we made each other *Speechless*.

After traveling the full sexual corridor from fucking to making love, I finally came to realize that Rick was really and truly a *top*. Even when I tried with my pinky finger to do you-know-what, you-know-where, he said, "Hell no! Put that where? Back there!" And in keeping his hetero-ways, he always paid for dinner, always bought the tickets, always drove, always bought expensive make-up gifts to get out of the dog house, and most importantly, he always, how can I say this, hmm, "ate a good meal before having dessert." Yes, Rick was the *top* I had desperately been looking for. We have now been luxuriating in a committed relationship for three months and it seems to get better each day. Next year, we are thinking of adopting a bottom for me on the side. It's amazing how great everything seems to be going considering how horrible things began.

Wendy, the only thing is, he has been having this recurring nightmare over the past few weeks that he has tried to avoid sharing with me. And recently, when I was going through his e-mail account (you know you gotta keep a tight leash on these men), I found out that the reason he doesn't want to share what happens in the nightmare is because in the nightmares the guy who attacked him, is me. So what should I do? I mean before he became my man I really wanted to tell him the truth. But now, I don't want to risk losing my relationship.

Wendy, I know you are busy being the Queen of All Media but I desperately need some of that great advice you give during your show. Please tell me how I can get out of this situation and keep my last chance for being with a real top. *I love you for listening.*

Yours Truly,
Crazy in Love

VERY PERCEPTIVE, PRACTICALLY PSYCHIC

Dear New York City,

    As my favorite cliché goes: "It's funny how time flies." Who could have imagined that I'd be employed by you for so many years? Honestly, it feels like only yesterday that I stuffed all of my belongings into the cheapest U-Haul truck I could afford and drove without so much as a quick glance in the rearview mirror to leave the city that no longer excited me, behind. And in that adrenalin-charged moment where I finally *appeared* in the city of big invisible apples, I remember how my mind bobbed in a barrel of questions: "*What will they think of me? What should they know about me? What shouldn't they know about me? Who was I before this moment? Who am I now? What will make me happy? What am I good at? Who do I want to become?*" Somehow over the course of and as a long-term spectator of time's aerobatic maneuvers, I often pretended the questions were rhetorical, answered them with half-answers and other questions, and ultimately decided that these questions didn't need answers at all—they required actions.

    To this day, I still don't totally believe all of my actions to the questions above, but as a result of working for you, I am now able to place most of my life into three categories: *who I am versus who I'm not, what I need versus what I want,* and *how I can live in my work as opposed to working to live.* You helped me to discover a unique set of skills (some hard, some soft), create a professional personality (not passive, not aggressive) and find a set of lifelong friends who keep me excited about the uncertainty of tomorrow. And as much as I have enjoyed all of the complicated bits of this relationship, it pains me to say that the time has come for us to part. Please consider this letter, my official letter of resignation effective "*Soon, 2000-Never.*" You see, Change's whisper has grown into a yell and it's profoundly clear that the only way to dull her refrain is by entering a new venue.

Best Regards,
Ready

PS

My partner, Donovan, and I have decided to move to Tushy-Screw, North Carolina, because he was just promoted to the second most senior executive position at his bank. As most of his regular business meetings will take place in North Carolina, it makes the most sense for us to relocate. We have been together almost five years now and we are truly excited about our transition from our one-bedroom Harlem apartment (that you generously provided complete with intelligent mice, dumb neighbors, and ever-increasing rent) to our five-bedroom, cul-de-sacked McMansion complete with cookie-cutter ingenuity and Martha Stewart charm. As an added bonus, we were recently reassured by the real estate agent that our new community is steadily becoming a gay-borhood for affluent same-gender couples. During our last visit, we had the pleasure of meeting a young lesbian couple—two former WNBA players—that will be our neighbors. They went on and on about their monthly cookouts as well as their keg and spades parties. I simply can't wait!

In other good news, almost simultaneously with the news of Don's promotion, we solidified our search for a surrogate and found a very nice (1600 on SAT, perfectly healthy, tall, perfect teeth, trilingual, ex-model) *Black* woman who has agreed to spend the last two months of her pregnancy in our new home in North Carolina. Don and I decided that we would use my sperm since a few of his brothers have had some issues with the law. However, I know he will love my baby, excuse me, our baby with all of his heart. Donovan, being a bit gay old school, has strongly urged me to be a stay-at-home papi for the first few years of our child's development. And after much consideration of his offer—monthly three-day spa vacations, daily cleaning service, one childfree dinner a week, and a quarterly all-expense paid shopping trip to NYC—I have decided to accept and temporarily leave my career in higher education. I am ecstatic about being a father and the amazing opportunity I will have to observe mini-me grow into the person we paid for. Tushy-Screw will actually allow me to raise a child in a gay-friendly environment without the everyday stresses that you have persistently provided during my tenure here.

And to be fair, even if I weren't soon to be raising a child, the constant stress and mental hustling you thrive on has really just become unnecessary in my life. In North Carolina, I won't have to fight overweight women for a seat on an overcrowded train, pretend like I am asleep to avoid barefoot vagrants begging for change, or listen to unruly children curse at each other just like their respective yet disrespectful parents did the night before. In North Carolina, I won't have to leave for and come home from work to be greeted by wayward adults sitting in front of my building, each grinning in the stench of brown-bagged liquor and postulating the endless ways that they can do less with their lives. In North Carolina, I won't have to go to a laundromat and waste hours washing and drying two loads, visit three different grocery stores to find my food for the week, nor will I have to worry about my mother being robbed by teenagers (more worried about the teenagers) when she and her girlfriends come to visit.

New York City, not to sound too gay (not that I really care) but I want to wake up to beauty. The smell of urine and feces as I wait for a consistently inconsistent train to take me to work, constantly stepping in random dog shit, and watching sleeping homeless people *everywhere* that not so gently remind you how the loss of your job could change even smarty pants *you* is just no longer tolerable. I want to wake up to the deafening silence of suburbia that slowly disappears with chipper *"Good mornings,"* *"Have a good days,"* and *"See you at the school fund-raisers."* I want to smell twice-a-week cut grass, long-leaf pine trees, homecooked breakfast, and school-bus exhaust fumes when I wake up. I want to see housewives and house-husbands washing cars, planting flowers, competing with each other for the unofficial crown for having the best outdoor Christmas lights, and showing each other pictures of the strangely uninteresting things they caught their children doing. I want to live some place where the police sirens and ambulance chants are so uncommon that everybody comes to the middle of the street to see what is going on. I want to live some place where good things and good people are actually the norm.

I hope you understand how much I have appreciated being part of your team as well as the personal development opportunities that I have been afforded. But as my second favorite cliché goes, "Enough is enough."

Dear Mr. Funeral Director,

The fact that you are reading this letter means that I am dead. Yes, I know you and the rest of the world are mourning, but I need you to pull it together and get to work. My *Departure Ceremonies,* which will include a pre-party, arts brunch, memorial service, and after burial party, will require quite a bit of planning. As there is absolutely no time to waste, over the next few paragraphs, I have provided a very specific set of deliverables for each activity. And don't even think about taking any creative liberties with my instructions. The lawyer who gave you this letter has clear marching orders to beat the hell out of you, sue you, and/or call my good friend Celeste—immortal/fierce ex-supermodel/drag queen/voodoo priestess living in the 7th Ward—to bring me *back* so that I can exact a delightful *Alien/Carrie/The Omen/TheRing/Saw* combination of revenge on your ass. I'm sure you will do just fine as you, really, don't have much of a choice. So let's get started!

The theme for the pre-party will be "Late 20th Century" fusing the '70s and the very late '90s. A down payment has been placed at the *Roxy* and *Generator* nightclubs. Based on feedback from my fans and loved ones, you will be able to decide which location is the most appropriate. When mourners enter the chosen location, I want them immediately overwhelmed by the smell of red currant Votivo candles. Their first sight should be that of topless female and *bottomless* male strippers. Please instruct them to skate joyfully to the sounds of Beyoncé and The BeeGees beneath the '70s imported golden disco ball. In honor of the date of my birth, I want each guest to take a flaming shot of Countreau on the 24th minute of every hour in conjunction with a light and smoke show where 10-feet-wide and 20-feet-long photographs of me are dramatically erected from beneath the *Saturday Night Fever* dance floor. Simultaneously, I want Bahamian stilt walkers to perform piqué turns around my erected images (ask Freud) with sparklers in their hands and glitter spewing from their mouths. Also, in honor of my trips to Amsterdam, Miami, Montreal and Rio, I want (for descendants of my whoring best friends and our many jump-offs) a clean co-ed dark room with VIP towel and condom service.

Additionally, *anybody* who attempts to do the cha-cha, electric, or any other type of slide must be tasered and evacuated from the club—*immediately.* Please know that my ignorant-ass-in-laws from my first two marriages might be there, and *chile*, don't even bother with the taser when they start "sliding" because it just...won't...work. They all have supernatural crackhead strength, especially when they're dancing. So, just in case, here is what you need to do: Tell one of the female strippers to skate by with a platter of rib tips, fried chicken, lemon pound cake, and a few cans of Budweiser beer. Once they spot her, they will charge her like a pack of bulls, so you have to make sure she can find her way to the roof quickly.

After the last foaming-mouth freak makes it to the roof, instruct her to get as close as possible to the edge and yell "FREE SOUL FOOD." She must then immediately throw the entire platter over the edge. As my first two husbands and their families are part wolf, they will be so outraged by the thought of wasting good soul food, they will jump after it, instantly killing themselves without the slightest bit of fear or regret. Give the stripper a few extra dollars and send her home for the night after she signs a confidentiality agreement. Sorry for the tangent, I just wanted to be clear. Anyway, when there are 10 minutes left until the last song will be played, find a way for all eight of the aforementioned photographs to explode into a stunning display of indoor multicolored fireworks. Like Prince's request for his guitar in the last scene of *Purple Rain*, I want the pictures to "cum." My last *young* husband, Anikan Nicholas Smith, should give a speech about how much I meant to him as the last photograph dazzles. And please help this boy with his diction, Lord knows his English "*no is good*" and it only gets worse when he is in a stressful situation. (Bless his Dominican heart).

The arts brunch should be hosted at the Alvin Ailey Dance studio in Manhattan. All guests should be asked to wear white with one light-lavender accessory to represent my fixation and lifelong affair with the movie *The Color Purple*. After an hour or so of three jazz harpists playing my favorite Nina Simone songs in the background, please ask that my guests be seated to watch scenes from my favorite movies. First, show *Jackie's Back* from beginning to end because there are just too many scenes that have turned a bad day good. Following that, you may select a few tear-jerker scenes from *The Color Purple, Cocoon, My Best Friend's Wedding, Notes on a Scandal, Mary Poppins, Dreamgirls, Black Orpheus, Mad Hot Ballroom, The Wiz,* and *The Thomas Crown Affair.* After the last clip has been shown, invite the guests to enjoy a light brunch consisting of rose Veuve Clicquot and all my favorite Thai and Pan-Asian dishes that have kept my milkshake bringing the boys to the yard. After everyone has consumed about $2,000 dollars worth of champagne and food, please have my adopted Indian son, Jukwan, speak about my love of dance, the Ailey institution, and the many performances I took him to see prior to him marrying that poor white trash girl named Honey. After his speech, the Ailey Dancers will perform choreography from *Episodes* and selected excerpts from the legendary work *Revelations* as guests pass one another the framed eight-by-ten foot by ten, black-and-white photograph used on the back cover of my 8th novel entitled "Ancient Gay Civilization: A Guide to Living Well in Your Fifties." Make sure to get the photograph back after the last person has adequate time to cry on it—you know how folks steal stuff and put it on *the* eBay.

Moving on... Please tell my hypermasculine professional football-playing son August that he and that nice (dark-skinneded) girl he married from Spelman will give remarks at my memorial. If she makes the mistake of referring to me as Dad as she sometimes does, feel free to slap the hell out of August. I told his ADHD having ass I don't like that heifer like that. At any rate, as I took much care to die on the exact day I was born 100 years ago, I want my memorial service to be a collection of readings from my favorite authors during each of my 10 decades of life. August will be able to pull this together as I have spent nearly $200,000 on educating him throughout his life only for his passion to consist of kicking an oval, caramelized pigskin up and down the 100-yard line. Really, its ok, I'm dead now. Plus, I took August's son, June, to Fashion Week last year for his third birthday. As June pointed and waved his index finger at the black models while shouting OVAH in his darling little voice, I realized that, oddly enough, August's life and mine would not be that different! (Evil Laugh)

Finally, even though I want the casket closed, I want to be laid to rest in gold aviator sunglasses and a hooded green linen caftan. As I rock my last high-fashion pose, if placed correctly, I should look just like I did for my first cover of *Men's Vogue*: my face should be pointing to heaven, my right hand placed behind my head creating a horizontal V, and my left hand hugging my right side, forcing my left elbow to point up to God. In my casket, please include my graduate-school diploma, the deed to my first house, Anikan's green card, and my first check where I made over six figures. All else, including my favorite teddy bear, Snuggles, will be bequeathed to my precious (light skinneded) grandson, June. Please find a descendant of Kenny Lattimore to sing *Well Done* acapella as I am lowered into the ground next to the love of my life—the inventor of red velvet cake.

After I am lowered into the ground and properly covered by dirt mixed with white rose petals and fuchsia orchids, please bring the African drummers out to begin the After Party. As they passionately beat their drums to a deep house rhythm, I want everybody to dance as if they are part of the Samba school I created during my annual trip to Carnival, some 45 years ago. The day will start off cloudy (negotiated with God for effect), but as people really get into the rhythms, and my grandson June starts to dance in his point shoes, the sun will shine like a spotlight on my family and fans as the warmest rain ever moisturizes their spirits with my love and care.

Once you see the sun, go grab Jukwan and kiss him in front of his wife. This will be the emotional awakening he needs to deal with his sexuality. His other daddy and I did not go through the trouble of raising him for his silly ass to be in the closet!

I'll be watching you from above!

Yours truly,
One Who Lived Well

CHAPTER SIX

Is It Me Or Is It New?

Dear New Year,

    I cannot remember a want (this strong) or a need (so desperate) as my craving for the advent of you. Even after taking popular antidepressants like Xanax and Absolut (Peach, Citrus, and my new favorite, Pear) for several months, I've come to realize that the only solution to the mélange of my problems (also known as issues) is for me to gently and aggressively embrace you. All of my extra estrogen has been put to great use: I made a fresh pot of black-eyed peas (using pork to ensure the authenticity), made a shrine next to my bed of beautiful stones (to wake up to pretty things in your presence), bought a small white dove (that I will set free when you arrive), bought a large yet personal bottle of vintage Veuve Clicquot, sautéed the greenest cabbage I could find, picked up my new winter-white outfit and yellow underwear, found my perfect 12 grapes, bought firecrackers to light (and throw at the dog next door that barks all damn night), and last, but certainly not least, I created a "Mr. Old Year" doll containing pictures, business cards, and old bank statements with all those pretty little ledgers containing "-$36.00" that I delicately tossed in extra virgin kerosene to ensure a rich and ashy hue as it sizzles in your honor.

    God knows, I am ready for your love. I'm eliminating- an all black x-tube, somebody to write a letter to Oprah on my behalf, a complete ban on cigarettes (and public caning of those who smoke them), five more paid holidays, the disappearance of my graduate school debt (yes, I'm being dramatic), and even my six-month stomach staple from my wish list in order to make sure all of my positive prayer energy is intently focused on you.

    Grab your noisemaker because I'm counting down until you unveil a happier me! *Ten* (or more) sexual experiences that probably didn't need to happen, *nine* take-out meals I bought when I was depressed, *eight* pounds that I loss and gained within a three-week period, *seven* strong-ass cocktails that assisted with this lists *Ten* spot, *six* people I allowed to really piss me off to the point where I was shaking, *five* books that I started and stopped, *four* days I laid in the bed without eating or showering, *three* things I forgot to do as part of my resolutions from last year, *two* men whose excuses I turned into facts, yet and still only *one* person to blame for the things that went wrong.

Pop the cork because I'm counting down! *Ten* days where I felt more fear than hope, *nine* opportunities to speak when I chose to be silent, *eight* times I thought porn was the answer to my sexual needs, *seven* ways I rewarded bad behavior, *six* months I spent trying to remember who I was, *five* days it took me to realize that you cannot find love, *four* lovers to realize what I—do, don't, not so much, and if I'm in the mood—like about sex, *three* months to realize that your boyfriends nickname should not be "headache," *two* hours of trying to reach my doctor for results to realize that it's not worth it, and *one* more day after the *fifth* to realize that you have to create it. *Ten* times I waited for him to love me the way I wanted him to love me, *nine* reasons why it would have been advantageous to be into the whole man/woman love thing, *eight* potential husbands became Judies, *seven* failed attempts to hang out with people my own age, *six* iterations of the same résumé created to land the perfect job, *five* times *four* plus *three* equals the number of résumés I mailed out on an average week in August, *two* jobs in one year, and *one* mouse too many in my apartment.

Play "Auld Lang Syne" because I am counting down! *10* thousand dollars saved and not shamefully spent on clothes, *9* more letters so that I can begin pitching this book, *8* months free of anyone I know who is dying, *7* days of vacation on a sunny nude-optional beach, *6* months of focused gym time, *5* new recipes perfected, *4* flawless dinner parties, *3* less friends infected with HIV than last year, *2* new hobbies, and *1* perfectly normal, attractive, mommy-approved man. *10* conversations that will change my life, *9* moments where I am thankful for being me, *8* consecutive days where I turn the TV off and read, *7* consecutive days of drinking eight glasses of water, *6* gifts from men without having to hint, *5* sexual encounters where it's all about me, *4* mornings where I watch the sunrise, *3* days where I don't talk on the phone at all, *2* moments where the world recognizes my genius, and 1 moment when the separation between me and God doesn't exist. **10** fits of laughter till it hurts, **9** moments of being held by an angel, **8** tears of joy, **7** hugs that make my knees buckle, **6** kisses that make my pain melt away, **5** days when I look far better than I feel, **4** meditations where I see the truth, **3** children to whom I bring joy, **2** impromptu vacations, and **1** completely healthy year.

Happy New Me!

Yours Truly,
Hopeful

Dear Empty Room,

Slow down. Where in the hell is my damn belt? "Exactly where you left it!" Mama would say. Chuckle. I miss her. I'll call her in the morning. Focus. Stop rushing. I need to organize my brain. Breathe. *He* will wait if I am five minutes late. It's good to be a little late. Fashionable or some shit. Whatever. This is stupid. Here I go again. Frantic for yet another pointless first date. Sigh. Ok, stop it. I really have to stop saying stuff like that. I know better. I have to create positive energy. Say it aloud. *I invite happiness into my world. I am open to this experience. I deserve to be happy. I am open to this experience.* Alright, take a deep breath. Exhale the fear. Much better now. Back to running late. Do I have everything? **Watch**–*check*; **Glasses**–*check*; **Wallet**–*check*; God, I hope he offers to pay. Wish I liked women. Seems so much easier. But then I'd definitely have to pay. Chuckle. Focus. Which shoe? Eh, these make me look like I'm trying too hard. And these make me look like I'm seventy. Fuck it. Where are my leather flip-flops? Thank God I got a good pedicure last weekend. Great. Vaseline and feet it is. **Shoes**–*check.*

Ok, come on. Which smell-good? Think. What am I giving today? I should try something subtle. Strong enough to make him curious. You know what they say, "If a man thinks that it smells good, he will want to learn whether or not it tastes good." Who the fuck is "they?" Chuckle. Anyway. Yes, that smells good but it is beyond common. Every homo in the world acts like it is their special scent. I'll wear it the next time I wear brown. More for fall weather anyway. Plus, it smells too sweet. I'm not giving sweet today. I'm horny. Simple formula. He pays for dinner. He says more than the average amount of the right shit. *We* will be getting naked immediately following his calculation of double-the-tax-and-round-up. I can be such a slut sometimes. Focus.

Not that cheap-ass scented oil either. It didn't last past three o'clock yesterday. I have to give sexy all night. Oh my God. Where is that sample from *Jeffrey*? Found it. Fierce. This smells good. Back-boots. Got to love the gay vernacular. Chuckle. Focus. Behind the ears. Across the neck. Around the wrists. Back of the knees. And ooh, just in case, a few good dabs on the Lucky Charms and the Honeycomb. Who says that? Chuckle. I'm not going to screw him on the first date. But what if I wait and find out the not-so-hard way that he is a bad lay? I can see it now. "I do" in front of *mama-nem* followed by some awkward display of horizontal affection. Solitary movie-perfect tear rolling out of my right tear duct. *End of the Line* moaned painfully by Nina Simone as the background music. Focus. I can be so damn dramatic sometimes. Haven't even been on one date with the bastard and already I'm talking about commitment ceremonies and irreconcilable differences. I'm crazy. Chuckle. Few more dabs on my neck. **Cologne**–*check.*

Ok for real. I have to leave now. Got to get the hell out of here. Which hat? Ok, fine. No time. No hat. One last look. Beard trimmed close. No noticeable nose hairs. Teeth flossed. Lips perfectly moisturized. Self-kiss. **Face**–*check.* Damn, wait. I need my exit music. Where is that CD? I hate when people come over and don't put my shit back where they found it. There it is. I love this album. *I hear you be the block but I'm the lights that keep the streets on.* Work Beyoncé. Jeans tight but no Chelsea bulge. Little bit of chest. No stomach. *Partner let me upgrade you, flip a new page, introduce you to some new things, Upgrade you.* I ain't got no freaking time to be "dutty-whining" in the mirror. Just till the end of the song. Alright, I look cute. **Clothes**–*check.* Unplug the iron. Turn the stereo off. Where are my fucking keys? Here we go a-damn-gain. Damn troll always hiding my shit when I need it. I'm about to scream. No time. There they are. And yes, irritating maternal voice in my head- Exactly where I left them. Chuckle. **Keys**–*check.*

Quick rehearsal. Thanks so much for inviting me out. You look great. How is work? Sounds like you are a very busy man. I've been enjoying the single life. Had a difficult break up. Now I'm just focused on some creative things. Yes, I write. Paint a little, too. Where are you from originally? Really, I've never been there. I've always wanted to go. How long do you plan on being in NYC? It would be nice to meet someone to settle down with. But I'm not looking for love. It will happen when it's right. What do you do for fun? That's really exciting. I'm very low maintenance. I keep my expectations of men low. Are you sure you don't want me to leave the tip? No really, next time it's on me. **Representative**–*check.*

Best Regards,
Never Alone

Dear Advisory Board,

As most of you know, I recently met this boy who has officially made me forget that I am bitter, sarcastic, judgmental, and eccentric as hell. Yes, I know most of you know me as the guy who will take your happy moment and—in the prettiest big-legged plié—shit on it. Or some of you know me as the younger version of your parents who will nag you until you either agree or concede—just to shut me the hell up. And of course, some of y'all know me as the bastard who always rocks one little accessory or ethnic outfit that nobody else has ever seen and provides interesting fodder for all of the gays regarding my true ethnicity and/or sexual label. But I don't think any of you have seen the person I feel like I'm about to become. And even if you have, it's been so long that it's probably going to take some real mental adjustment. Yes, love muffins, I think I'm falling in love. (HELP!)

He is best described as *another* old soul with real charisma and proper grooming. Zagat's would describe him as "an unassuming new venue with great customer service, thoughtful presentation, and unlimited possibilities." During our first meal together, before a menu was even placed in our hands, he said, "Dinner is on me!" And as you can kind of imagine, based on my track record with cheap men, I politely went to the bathroom and got into one ole Holy Ghost filled Pentecostal shout session (SHEA BUTTA OH SHEA BUTTA). When I returned, he had already ordered an appetizer for us. And that was the first time I think I really "saw" him. Like most times when I meet people, I just go through the elevator speech and pay them little to no mind. I get through the "where you from?" "what you do?" "what do you do for fun?" and other monotonous questions, but I am never happily inspired to go and dig deeper. But when he started off by slapping me with his maturity and good manners, I decided that he was worth a few mind games and loaded questions to reprove my theory of "Most men ain't shit." But you know what, to my reluctant surprise, he didn't give me one "representative" answer and surprised me with his detail and elaboration. So after he passed almost every fail-proof test, and even flipped a few of the questions on me, I pulled out my glasses from my man purse and desperately tried to clean the lenses. By the time we ordered dessert, with my glasses clean and my heart oddly unfoggy, I saw him. And more importantly, not only did I see him but I "saw" me looking at him.

He reminds me of the first time I met a boy that I liked in high school. The unnecessary but absolutely required phone conversations into the wee hours of the morning, the silly jokes that are only funny to you and he, and the sharing of every little detail of life that nobody else cares about. It's totally juvenile and yet at the same time really grown-up. Like who knew you could actually enjoy talking to somebody your own age, in your own industry, and in your own city? Certainly not me.

And what's really great is that we have so much in common. He was raised in a very religious environment and I was raised by people who cussed religiously—this is how we both learned the power of words. I was taught that you had to "think ahead" when considering the complexion of your mate and he was taught that he could be anybody or anything he wanted because of his hue—we both are aware that we are light-"skinneded." He used to be a swimmer and I used to be a dancer—so we both have great legs and are self-conscious about the hard-core body fat that comes after the words, "I used to...." And right now, the only huge difference I noticed is that he has Capricorn discipline and I have Virgo omnipotence, which basically means I know he will have to be the one to make up the bed in the morning. Y'all, this boy has Minnie Riperton's *Simple Things* on repeat in my mind.

I'm trying really hard to relax and go with the flow. I mean, despite the fact that I have started picking out commitment ceremony invitations and figuring out which Third World country we will adopt our baby from, I have really just been taking things slow. No matter what you think, I did *not* juxtapose our hyphenated last names on my notepad at work nor did I dream about our monogrammed bath towels in our guest home in Miami. And for the record, I haven't thought about any of the ways we can build our wealth, grow old together, and have a normal and healthy commitment. Trust me, I'm just taking it slow. The only thing I have done is been really open, honest, and available. I haven't even told him that I think he's made me forget about anything other than the slice of heaven I found in him. Hell, I don't think I have even found the courage to admit it to myself. (Smile)

I'm just here y'all—in a place that I haven't been in a long time. It isn't sex clouding my judgment because we ain't had none. It isn't loneliness because I finally learned how to distinguish that emotion from being alone. It's not one-sided because he reciprocates and compliments every invitation, phone call, e-mail, and action I throw his way. What is it or as JJ from *Good Times* would say, "What it is"—I don't know. Maybe the universe realized how much I have grown since my last relationship and decided that its time for me to have the addition in my life that will grow me and challenge me to be vulnerable and unselfish once again. The right time? The right one? The right place? I think and instinctively believe that I have entered the beginning stages of a substantial and sincere love.

Yours truly,
Dreaming Wide Awake

PS
Stay tuned and please know that if this doesn't work out this letter will self-destruct!

I S I T M E O R I S I T N E W ?

Dear Good Morning,

I can't believe how
it felt to see you again.
Where did my pain hide? (1)

Is this really me
feeling lighter than before?
Wait, I just found new. (2)

Wide awake for this
to make my sad, my feel good.
Were my eyes, just closed? (3)

I don't take no shit
from no man who wants my love.
Just used to the smell. (16)

I'm not desperate
to have nobody around.
Just a bit lonely. (17)

Don't you fucking dare
think you all that and some dick.
Just be what I need. (18)

Listen to my laugh
and watch my eyes as they glow.
Who doesn't love new? (4)

Am I that crazy
because I think this will last?
This was made from scratch. (5)

Why can I feel you
when your name runs cross my mind?
Have the sense to stay. (6)

You know I like it
when you work your tongue like that.
Don't ask for days off. (19)

Stop, I can't take it
when you make it talk to me.
Such a dirty mouth. (20)

Damn boy, I'm tripping
from your sexy motor skills.
Fuck the brakes. Faster. (21)

I prepared a meal
with all of your favorites.
Guess what's for dessert. (7)

I ran you a bath
since your day was rough at work.
That's what I'm here for. (8)

Baby, it's okay
I'll just wash your clothes with mine.
I know. Back at new. (9)

Your hands and my legs
nothing appears separate
I'm falling in deep. (22)

Once out, now I'm in
everything has become clear
My heart is throbbing. (23)

Dizzy, here it comes
some things win the fight with change
My body explodes. (24)

After work, meet me
magnetized to your newness
Screw the playing field. (10)

These are my best friends
needy but not obsessive
Jury of your peers. (11)

Been waiting for this
balance between brain and heart
Moment of reckoning. (12)

Shower tomorrow
Still in the experience
Enjoy our right now (25)

Dreams are connected
Peaceful waves of consciousness
Cuddle at all times (26)

Cuter than before
Our morning words are awkward
Silence anxiety (27)

At last, votes are in
We to you; One us to them;
I feel new, again. (13)

Commitment and truth
Silly phone calls to say "hi"
The need to be there (14)

A new love is born
Innocent and free of lies
Believe it will last. (15)

Sneak behind you. Squeeze.
Surprising me with sunrise.
Starting the day right. (28)

I'll get in with you
Stop, the water will get cold
Giggle, fine let it. (29)

Pour love to the top.
Seriously, I like pulp.
Look, now it's half full (30)

Yours truly,
Feeling Haikus

Acknowledgements

I'd like to express gratitude to a few very special folks in my life such as Natalie (Yes, Kerry Washington will play you in the *Lifetime* movie version of my life), Julius, Kentay, Cisco, Fabian, Sam *(Samiranda)*, Allen *(Gay Grandpa)*, Robert *(Sandzie)*, Demarcus, Clarence Haynes, Wade *(My First Fan)*, Piter *(Literary Huz)*, McKelvin *(You're Just a Wannabe)*, CJ Southerland, Lisa Van Putten, Edith Bailey, Michael H., Chris Curse *(My Neck, My Back)*, Tiffany S., David Mensah, Susan E.(Somehow, You are Still My Having My Children), Dana, Arlyce P., Mr. Bibb *(Furball Delight)*, Dr. Vinnie, Vaughn, Savoy, Everett, Flores, James, Vernon *(Hollywood)*, Rex, and Melvin (*Buenos días*). Thank you all for believing in my work before I did.

To my family, thank you for loving me unconditionally and for providing a safe environment in which I could learn, grow, and most importantly, create.

To Mr. Clarence V. Reynolds, as I still have nightmares about those red symbols on the first draft of *Ready to Male*. I am convinced you are the most talented and thorough copyeditor on the planet. But next time, can you "utilize" a more writer-friendly color? The red pencil does somehow make me want to fight you.

To M.D.F., P.A.A., and M.J.M.—I Love you.

ABOUT THE AUTHOR

This is Lamar Ariel's first published work of autobiographical fiction.

Lamar Ariel currently resides in Manhattan where he works at _____ as a _____ . At twenty-something years old, Lamar Ariel is not straight, not white, not uneducated, and—contrary to popular opinion—not unusual. However, he is pro-creative and enjoys _____ while _____ at his home as well as the homes of those who let him. Due to the overwhelming success of *Ready to Male*, he is working on a second collection of letters that is uniquely entitled, *Ready to Male: Part Two*.

Printed in the United States
205247BV00002B/106-195/P